"You don't have to tell me," Niccolo murmured. "I can see it written on your face."

"See what? I have no idea *at all* what you're talking about."

"Liar."

"This is crazy. *You're my potential client!* I have no idea why we're talking about this!" Ellie's arms should have been pushing him aside and her legs should have been carrying her resolutely into the car, but instead she hovered, staring dry-mouthed at him.

"I don't... I'm not... Yes, you're an attractive man, *as well you know*, but I'm not, *definitely not*, attracted to you!"

The silence thrummed between them. He was going to kiss her. Her eyelids fluttered. Her whole body was tensed in a state of rigid suspension and a dark, forbidden excitement drummed through her veins.

"My mistake, in that case." Niccolo flipped down the sunglasses and stepped aside. For a few painfully long seconds Ellie couldn't move, then her breathing returned to normal.

Relieved. That's what she should be feeling, she told herself fiercely. She definitely shouldn't be feeling disappointment! She should be *relieved* that he had taken the hint. He wasn't her type. She didn't welcome his flirtatious advances! She wasn't attracted to him. Not really...

Cathy Williams can remember reading Harlequin books as a teenager, and now that she is writing them, she remains an avid fan. For her, there is nothing like creating romantic stories and engaging plots, and each and every book is a new adventure. Cathy lives in London, and her three daughters—Charlotte, Olivia and Emma—have always been, and continue to be, the greatest inspirations in her life.

Books by Cathy Williams

Harlequin Presents

Legacy of His Revenge
Cipriani's Innocent Captive
The Secret Sanchez Heir
Bought to Wear the Billionaire's Ring
Snowbound with His Innocent Temptation
A Virgin for Vasquez
Seduced into Her Boss's Service
The Wedding Night Debt
A Pawn in the Playboy's Game
At Her Boss's Pleasure
The Real Romero

The Italian Titans

Wearing the De Angelis Ring
The Surprise De Angelis Baby

One Night With Consequences

Bound by the Billionaire's Baby

Visit the Author Profile page
at Harlequin.com for more titles.

Cathy Williams

A DEAL FOR HER INNOCENCE

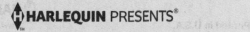

Recycling programs for this product may not exist in your area.

ISBN-13: 978-1-335-50417-3

A Deal for Her Innocence

First North American Publication 2018

Printed in U.S.A.

www.Harlequin.com

A DEAL FOR HER INNOCENCE

To my three wonderful and inspiring daughters.

CHAPTER ONE

'MR ROSSI IS in the gym.' The cool, blonde beauty manning the desk in the six-storeyed glass house that comprised the European headquarters of Niccolo Rossi's sprawling empire glanced up from the computer in front of her. Her face didn't crack a smile.

'The gym?' Had she got the day wrong? 'But I have an appointment,' Ellie said, hand tightening on the briefcase clamped to her side.

'Lower level, and the lifts are to the left,' the glacial beauty said, tapping one long, scarlet fingernail on the marble counter. 'He's expecting you. He has allotted you twenty minutes. He's a very busy man.'

Ellie's lips thinned. Reading between the lines, the message was loud and clear: *Get a move on, because time is money for the billionaire Niccolo Rossi, and you should consider yourself lucky that he's granted you an audience at all.*

Ellie wondered if acting as a barrier between her billionaire boss and the outside world was part of the woman's duties. Probably. Niccolo Rossi came with an extensive reputation as a ruthless playboy with a penchant for catwalk models and short-term relationships. The sort of man who had fun with women and, the second the fun was over, dropped them like a hot potato and moved on to the next one.

Only a month ago, she had been flicking through a weekly gossip rag, and there had been a telling picture of a stunning woman hiding behind a pair of over-sized sunglasses, the bold caption implying that she didn't want the world to see her distraught, puffy eyes in the wake of a cruel break-up.

Niccolo Rossi probably *needed* a Rottweiler at the front desk making sure distraught, puffy-eyed exes didn't get through to his inner sanctum.

Ellie had never met the man in the flesh but it didn't take a genius to figure out the sort of person he was. Young, rich and powerful. Good-looking as well, if you went for the traditional Italian type. Heavy on phoney charm, light on sincerity.

The kind of guy who didn't give a hoot about other people, which was why Ellie was now having to conduct her meeting with him in a gym, and with one eye on her watch, because time wasn't going to be on her side.

Hardly ideal. But then conducting this meeting on her own was hardly ideal either, even though she had talked herself into handling the pitch. She had a great record for winning work, she had secured two record, large clients, which had been a real boost, and she'd wanted to prove her worth to herself and to the other two partners in the small start-up advertising agency, in which they were joint investors, by winning this solid-gold client. She had used every scrap of the small inheritance left to her by a grandparent she had never met and had borrowed to meet the remainder of her contribution. She was an equal partner with an equal voice, but she was younger and less experienced, and still felt that there was a ladder to climb before she was on a par with her two other partners.

This was to be the feather in her cap, but Stephen would still accompany her for gravitas, although his role would be to sit back and watch and field any awkward questions. His role, unfortunately, had bitten the dust when his mother had been rushed to hospital the evening before. Right now, Stephen Prost was on bedside vigil and Adam, the other partner in the agency, couldn't possibly abandon ship to hold her hand.

'I don't need my hand to be held!' Ellie had reassured him with glowing confidence.

However, that was before she had been faced with the change of venue and a stopwatch.

She thought of the painstaking work she had put in on the advertising campaign for Niccolo Rossi. She had worked even longer hours than she usually did because this job was beyond big. She had sourced every available scrap of information she could on his boutique resort in the Caribbean, which hardly needed any outside help when it came to getting noticed. She had spent endless hours, way into the night, thinking of creative ways to sell the resort to the mega-rich audience he wanted to attract.

And now she was being granted twenty minutes while the big man ran on a treadmill with one headphone in his ear, making a pretence of listening to what she had to say. She didn't think that the other big players in advertising tendering for the job had pitched to him sitting on a yoga mat in a gym. No chance.

The heat of the gym hit her like a solid brick wall the second she pushed open the glass door. Her eyes skittered over the fearsome array of machines, the punch bags to one side, the unforgiving mirrored wall, and finally came to rest on the single sweating male in the room lifting a stack of weights that literally made her wince.

Niccolo Rossi.

He looked nothing like the grainy images she had occasionally glimpsed of him in the past. For a start, in all those grainy images he had been fully dressed. Here, in the gym, he was in a black tee shirt and a pair of shorts, standing with his back to her, his lean, bronzed body rippling with taut muscle as he slowly hefted the bar with its impossible load, from ground to waist, and from waist to shoulder, then up. His skin gleamed with sweat.

Mesmerised, Ellie could do little more than just hover in the doorway and stare.

Still in her coat, she could feel perspiration trickling down her back.

She was dressed for a cold winter day. Barely there black tights, black skirt, neat white blouse, not quite buttoned to the neck but almost, and black pumps. She was dressed for a meeting in a boardroom with men in suits and a whiteboard safely tucked away somewhere in the background. Here, in this testosterone-charged space, she felt ridiculous in her neat work outfit, clutching her briefcase.

Consummate professional that she was, Ellie was irritated with herself for the lapse in focus.

She was here to do a job. True, she would have wanted more time than the scant twenty, probably now fifteen, minutes she had been allocated, but she was smart enough to filter out all unnecessary information and still work to her brief. She had no choice.

There were hard copies of everything anyway. She never pitched for any job without meticulous preparation and she never, ever relied on her clients remembering everything she said. It always paid dividends to make sure they had all the information to hand by way of something both tangible and in email format.

Hard copy *anything* felt superfluous here.

Straightening, she took a deep breath and walked towards Niccolo.

Her shoes clicked briskly on the hardwood floor and, if he hadn't been aware of her existence before, he was now, because he dropped the weights on the mat with a resounding crash that made her jump.

He turned round slowly and Ellie stopped. Her heart had vacated her chest and migrated to somewhere in her mouth, which had gone dry. The blood running through her veins had turned to molten lava. Her thoughts had suddenly become scrambled and a deep fog had settled over her brain. The man was beauty in motion, his body slick, his slightly long, dark hair damp with sweat.

Eyes as dark as night registered her as she stood in front of him, clutching her briefcase for dear life, and fit to explode from the heat in the sensible coat which she hadn't thought to remove.

He had the lushest lashes she had ever seen on a man, long, thick and fringing eyes that were, just for a few seconds, veiled of all expression.

His features were chiselled to perfection. She knew that he was part-Italian but, unless one was standing right in front of him, it was hard to tell from a picture just *how* exotic that ancient thread of ancestry was. He wasn't just your typical tall, dark and good-looking guy. He was a one-of-a-kind *dangerously* tall, dark and good-looking guy. He oozed the sort of blatant, uncompromising sex appeal that made women walk into lamp posts.

'Eleanor Wilson.' Ellie rushed into frantically confused speech, thoroughly disconcerted by the effect he was having on her and not caring for it at all. '*Ms.*'

The veiled expression cleared and his dark, dark eyes connected with hers with a hint of amusement.

'*Ms* Eleanor Wilson,' he drawled, reaching

down for a towel she hadn't noticed and wiping his face before slinging it over his shoulders. He looked at her from her head down, then back up again, then he made an elaborate show of peering around her. 'Where are the rest of you?'

'Just me, I'm afraid. Stephen Prost, my business partner, is dealing with a personal emergency at the moment. I hope you won't mind me saying, but I wasn't expecting to have to discuss my pitch in a gym. Would we be able to find a seat somewhere?' She looked around her and failed to see anywhere that could remotely work for her to show him what she had brought with her unless she opted for doing her spiel on the treadmill.

Annoyance flared. How hard was it to stick to the rule book? He had made an appointment, and surely he could at the very least have the courtesy to honour the commitment he had made?

She pursed her lips, bristling. Rules and regulations were in place for a reason. The work place and life in general only operated smoothly if all parties concerned took time out to respect one another.

'You should take the coat off,' Niccolo said gently. 'You must be very hot.'

'I hadn't expected to be in a gym,' Ellie repeated with a tight smile.

'And so now you are.' Niccolo shrugged. 'You have to roll with the punches. Follow me.' He spun round and began walking towards the back of the gym.

Changing rooms. He was heading to the changing rooms. She could see a concealed door. Ellie cast a desperate glance behind her to the door through which she had come, while her legs propelled her behind him, towards a scenario that took her so far out of her comfort zone that she felt faint.

Ellie behaved by the rules and she believed in them. It was just the way she was. She liked them. She liked the sense of order they conferred. She had lived a peripatetic life with her wandering, nomadic, hippy parents. She had spent a childhood that had spanned the continents, from India as a toddler, through Australia with a brief stint in New Zealand, before returning to Europe via Ibiza, Greece and Spain. She had barely seen the inside of any schools because nothing as dull and as institutional as a school had been allowed to cloud the endlessly blue horizons of her free-spirited parents. Routine had been their enemy and she had become the unwitting victim of their scatty, idealised belief system.

For Ellie, being on the move had fostered a deeply ingrained desire for stability.

By the time her feet had hit the ground at fourteen, and her parents had ruefully accepted that their thirst to see every corner of the globe had been sufficiently quenched, Ellie had thrown herself into the joy of *going nowhere* with a passion that had almost been physical.

She was a stickler for detail but with a creative streak that had been passed down from her arty parents. That combination had won her her first job at a major advertising agency and, from there, she had been invited to take a chance and team up with Stephen and Adam, both ambitious CEOs at the same firm, to form their fledgling agency. It was the biggest risk she had ever taken, and she had taken it after careful consideration, because she had felt confident about their prospects at capturing a niche but significant market with a media-savvy audience. Everything she did was done with consideration, with nothing left to chance. Like the portfolio she was clutching. A portfolio that should have been displayed in the sanitised confines of a designated office space. With the whiteboard. And no treadmills or punch bags in sight.

She eyed Niccolo's muscled torso as his T-shirt clung to it, the length of his legs, the strength of his arms, the powerful ripple of muscle and sinew, and she shivered. Here was a man who scorned rules and regulations, and now she wondered just how she was supposed to form any sort of rapport with a man who thought nothing of conducting a meeting in a gym. In the world of advertising, rapport was top dog.

Worse. He was now going to conduct his meeting in the changing rooms of a gym.

He opened the door and she shrieked to a stop, nerves all over the place, fingers grasping the briefcase until her knuckles were white.

Niccolo turned around, both hands on the ends of the towel looped over his shoulders.

Under normal circumstances, this was not the venue he would have chosen to conduct a meeting, but he had reached his office later than normal. Eight instead of his usual six.

He had also not been in the best of moods. His last lover had embarked on on a kiss-and-tell rampage in the press after he had broken off their relationship, and his mother and three sisters had seen fit to link arms in a united front, their mission being to subject him to full-frontal verbal assault on his colourful love life.

Where he had gone to see his mother for dinner at her exquisite cottage near Oxford, expecting some light chat and the usually excellent food her private chef was summoned to provide whenever there were guests, he had instead found himself in the company of not just his mother but his three sisters.

Each of whom had very strong opinions on the sort of women he dated.

He had consequently overslept, and the only thing he had wanted to do when he'd reached his office was to work off some of his stress in the company of a punch bag and a gruelling set of weights.

And, in fairness, he hadn't expected a woman. And certainly not a woman who looked as though she sucked on lemons for fun.

Right now, she was staring at him with a mixture of disapproval and consternation.

Her coat was still on and her brown hair was neatly scraped back into a bun. A pair of heavy spectacles would have transformed her into the archetypal school mistress.

Although, he had to concede, her eyes were a rather interesting shade of hazel and her mouth, dragged into an unforgiving thin line at the moment, could be quite attractive, because her lips were full and pink.

'You've stopped,' he said politely. 'Why have you stopped?'

'I'm afraid I really don't think it appropriate for me to have a business meeting with you in a changing room.'

'Oh, dear. As you can see, I'm currently not in my suit, and after an hour and a half in this place I really need to get out of my sweaty gear.'

Two bright patches of hot colour had appeared in her cheeks. Her skin tingled as though she was standing too close to an open flame and, in response to those physical responses, she found herself clutching the briefcase ever harder.

He was lounging against the doorframe with the door only partially open behind him.

'Perhaps I could wait for you in your office,' Ellie suggested. She stared at his face, because it seemed the safest place to rest her eyes—the other option being his barely clothed body—but he was so stunningly beautiful that he brought her out in a cold sweat. She desperately wanted to ignore his superior height and the powerful perfection of his muscular frame but it was like trying to ignore a tsunami.

'Perhaps you could…' Niccolo mused, eyes firmly focused on her heart-shaped face, which was awash with uncomfortable colour. 'But no. I'm afraid not. I haven't got enough time to spare.' He straightened. 'If the account means anything to your agency, then regrettably you're going to have to get past your discomfort with my inappropriate behaviour and follow me.' He grinned and raised his eyebrows, waiting for her response.

'This—this is highly unconventional,' Ellie stuttered in a last-ditch attempt to stay on the safe side of the partially opened door.

'Stickler for convention?' Niccolo asked, tilting his head to one side and allowing the silence to trickle between them like an electric current.

'Yes.' Ellie didn't hesitate to set him straight on that score. If there was one thing her eternally unconventional parents had taught her, it was the value of convention.

Niccolo laughed with genuine amusement. How old was she? Somewhere in her twenties, but she dressed like a woman in her fifties, and that prissy approach was more reminiscent of a granny laying down laws than a young woman working in the exciting, hot-shot world of advertising.

The other contenders he had interviewed briefly for this assignment had been trendy to the point of wearisome. Hats, beards and wire-rimmed spectacles on the men and painfully cutting-edge outfits on the women. He didn't think any of them would have been fazed at having to conduct their interview in a gym. He suspected that the women would have actively enjoyed the experience.

This particular woman looked as though the experience was on a par with being locked in a room with a dangerous airborne virus.

In a world that was largely predictable, Niccolo found that he was beginning to enjoy himself.

'Well, at least you're honest,' he observed. 'Although, I confess I'm not at my best when I'm around people who tether themselves to rules and regulations. I like people who can think out of the box.'

'I'm a great believer in rules and regulations.' Ellie's mouth tightened, nostrils flaring as she breathed in the heady musk of his masculine scent. Her eyes were drawn to the V of his black tee shirt and then lingered. The tee shirt was tight enough to accentuate the hard width of his chest and the tapering slimness of his waist. She could glimpse some dark hair just where the V of the tee shirt ended, and it was so strangely and intensely masculine a sight that her breath hitched in her throat for a few shocking seconds, then she hurriedly looked away, heart hammering like a sledge hammer inside her chest.

'But...' she breathed deeply, steadying the sudden race of her pulses '...that's not to say that I don't think out of the box.' She visibly relaxed as some of her wildly scattered thoughts began to cohere into the little rehearsed speech she had mentally prepared on her way to his office. 'I'm excellent when it comes to creating the sort of dynamic a client is looking for in their advertising campaigns. In case you're not aware of it, we might be a small firm, and relative newcomers to the scene, but we're incredibly dynamic and as such we know how to connect with a young market. Social media in all its various forms is the prime tool when it comes to a successful pitch, and we pride ourselves on being top of the game in that area.'

'Thank you for the spiel,' Niccolo said politely, pushing himself away from the door. 'But I still need to change. You can carry on trying to win my business while I freshen up.' He swung round and carried on talking over his shoulder while Ellie followed on wobbly legs, eyes pinned to his back as he led the way into a spacious room, tiled from floor to ceiling in white-and-grey marble with two of the walls mirrored so that unfortunately her reflection was thrown back at her from every angle.

Ellie did her best to ignore the sight of herself. She was five-foot-six but, even with her heels elevating her by a couple of inches, he still towered over her.

A fleeting glimpse of their reflections in

the daunting mirrored walls as they walked through the outer room made her heart sink.

He'd said that he wasn't at his best with people who *'tether themselves to rules and regulations'*. He'd made it sound as though anyone who wasn't an out-and-out maverick was a crashing bore and of no interest.

What must he think of her, in that case? She'd already pinned her colours to the mast when it came to rule-breaking and, if she hadn't, then one look at her would have convinced him that she was just the sort of dreary, conventional bore he would never be at his best with.

If he was the equivalent of a dangerous, wildly unpredictable and outrageously beautiful jungle cat, then she was the equivalent of the fearful sparrow sitting on the branch of a tree, making damned sure not to get too close.

Her clothes were neat and, she knew, uninspiring. Her figure was likewise neat and uninspiring. She possessed neither the curves of the sex bomb nor the androgynous skinny chic of the model. She was just...slender. Her breasts had never been big enough, as far as she was concerned. Her shoulder-length hair, scraped back into a utilitarian chignon at the nape of her neck, was shiny and glossy but... brown. She had her own niche market of clients who were reassured by her competence and straightforward, intelligent approach, impressed by her careful meticulousness and charmed by the flashes of wit and verve she brought to all her campaigns. Niccolo Rossi wasn't going to be one of these reassured, impressed or charmed clients.

She was never going to win this contract. You really had to bond with the person on the opposite side of the fence when it came to winning a contract. You had to be singing from the same song sheet or else they would never trust that you would be able to perform in the manner they wanted. It was all a very subjective process.

An unpredictable jungle cat and a little brown sparrow did not make natural bed partners.

Already contemplating the prospect of failure, and trying to work out how it might impact on the fortunes of the agency, Ellie didn't notice that they had exited the marble outer room and were now in the changing rooms, which were also tiled in marble, but unfortunately not quite so impersonal, because the bank of showers suggested, all too clearly, just how intimate the space was.

She froze.

The colour drained from her cheeks.

She was still in her coat, and practically passing out from the heat, but too embarrassed to remove it in a place like this, which was specifically designed for the removal of clothing.

Niccolo folded his arms and looked at her. Never had he seen a face so expressive of a rabbit suddenly staring into the harsh, bright glare of oncoming headlights.

He marvelled that she worked in the cutthroat world of advertising at all and, more than that, was an active partner in the small but, he knew, talented advertising agency which she represented.

'I would not normally be conducting business here,' he felt constrained to tell her, even though it wasn't in his nature to explain himself to anyone. 'Unfortunately, I got into work much later than I normally do.' He grimaced as he thought of the four delightful harridans laying into him the evening before. 'Not your fault, I do realise, but I decided, once I got here that I had to hit the gym. Unfortunately, it happened to coincide with your appointment, which I should, in retrospect, have cancelled.'

'No!' Ellie was quick to respond. 'It's perfectly fine. A little unusual, of course, but...'

'But I'm a billionaire and your agency is desperate to get its hands on this assignment, so having to put up with *inappropriate behav-*

iour from the head of the company is a pill you're willing to swallow for the greater good.' He grinned, folded his arms and stared at her for a few moments, then he turned away and disappeared behind a wall. She could still hear him, though, just as she could hear the rush of water as the shower was turned on.

Her twenty minutes were surely up, and she had shown him nothing of what she had done. But then, he'd probably made up his mind anyway, so wasn't particularly interested in seeing her work.

Frankly, she could leave right now, but it somehow seemed rude to slink away while his back was turned.

While he was in the shower.

Naked.

Ellie suddenly found herself in the grip of a level of imagination she'd never known she possessed. She pictured him under the running water, lathering his big, powerful body with soap, face upturned. He wasn't one of those metrosexual guys with spindly legs and hairless chests. He was aggressively, belligerently male and his dark, dangerous in-your-face sex appeal made her giddy and flustered.

'You've gone silent on me,' Niccolo drawled, emerging from the concealed cubicle, trousers on, lazily doing up the buttons on his shirt.

Ellie blinked and then reddened as she recalled the graphic images of him that had sent her blood pressure soaring.

He was decent, and for that she was immeasurably grateful. Grey trousers and a white shirt. Barefoot, though, and his hair was still damp from the shower.

'Time's not on your side, Ms Eleanor Wilson. In actual fact—' he glanced at the expensive watch on his wrist '—your twenty minutes was up five minutes ago but, considering you didn't cater for having to do your pitch in the company gym, I'm going to extend your time for a further half an hour. Think you'll be able to do what you came here to do in that time? Provided you don't spend any more of it staring at me. And, for God's sake, take the coat off. The last thing I need is to waste my morning pandering to a damsel in distress who's passed out because she's overheated.'

Ellie didn't have time to say anything in response to this because he was already walking out of the changing rooms towards yet another door which she hadn't noticed before. It led directly out to a comfortable wooden-floored room equipped with everything anyone might want after a gruelling workout.

A refrigerated glass cooler held bottles of water and energy drinks, and fruit, energy bars and healthy protein snacks filled deep trays on a counter. No one was serving and it was obvious that the generous contents of the canteen were open to any employee choosing to use the gym.

Niccolo grabbed a bottle of mineral water and proceeded to drink it in one long swallow.

For a few seconds, Ellie was mesmerised by the brown column of his throat as he finished the water, then, galvanised into action, she whipped off the offending coat and quickly pulled out her tablet and all the documentation she had brought with her.

If all she had was half an hour, then she was determined to stuff it as full as she possibly could with the mock-ups she had brought with her.

'There are hard copies of everything,' she began, remaining on her feet while he sat on one chair and dragged another towards him so that he could use it as a makeshift foot-rest. He relaxed back, hands linked loosely behind his head, and watched as she fumbled with the mound of paperwork she had brought with her. Her tablet was already up and running.

She was the epitome of efficiency. The coat had been discarded to reveal an outfit as bland as he had expected. Now that she wasn't having to try and evade the sight of him in a sweaty tee shirt and the loose jersey shorts he wore whenever he worked out in the gym, she had reverted to the brisk professional she undoubtedly was.

Niccolo harked back to the delicately blushing cheeks and the awkward discomfort and thought it was a shame that she was morphing into just the sort of career woman he was so accustomed to dealing with. He'd quite liked the delicately blushing cheeks and the awkward discomfort. Professional, efficient career women were a dime a dozen. As were practised, seductive temptresses, and he should know, because he'd dated enough of them in the past.

A woman who blushed, though, was as rare as hen's teeth and Niccolo had enjoyed the sight.

On cue, she was delivering her talk about the hotel complex that was to be the subject of the advertising campaign. She'd done her research very thoroughly indeed, that much was obvious. She seemed to know more about his own hotel complex than he did, but then this foray into the world of leisure was a departure from his usual conquests.

His path to fame, glory and riches had started in the highly profitable maze of apps. He'd had a special talent for spotting the startups that were going to go stellar and he had known how and when to invest. He'd been a millionaire almost before leaving university with his first-class degree in computer engineering and maths. He'd turned that million into several more when he'd started acquiring ailing companies and spinning them into gold mines, and the millions had become billions as his reach had extended. But he'd never thought about the leisure industry until one of his sisters had mentioned something about how tough it could be finding the right life-partner.

Niccolo didn't believe in partners, right or otherwise. He believed in the purity of work. But he'd had experience from way back when of a match-making app that had taken off and he had spotted the chance to combine known territory with the interesting and as yet unexplored avenue of high-end hotels, and thereby add to his already considerable fortune. Why not? The fantasy of love wasn't for him, for a number of reasons, but that didn't mean that it didn't exist, and he was very happy to provide the wherewithal for all those hopefuls in search of their happy-ever-after dream.

Niccolo had had his future mapped out from the day his father had died. At the time, he had been only eight but, as his father had told him on his death bed, he was now the man of the house and would have to step up to the plate.

Niccolo could not remember a time when he hadn't been aware of the importance of working to make sure his family were taken care of. By the time he hit twenty-one, fresh out of Cambridge University, the family company had been on its last legs.

The thorny business of wondering what direction to take with his life had never crossed his radar because he'd known from a kid where his destiny lay. Duty above all else. The mantra had lodged in his head in his dying father's message. In one hand, he'd juggled with the demands of revamping his family business, while in the other he'd developed his breath-taking skills in the fast-moving world of technology, learning over time how to link the two. He'd grown up fast because he had moved straight from university life into the cut-throat world of the men in suits who ran the financial markets.

Niccolo assumed that he had known innocent young women who blushed but, if he had, then it had been a long time ago. Now, with billions at his disposal and a social circle that included some of the most powerful movers and shakers on the planet, the women he met had left their blushing days a long time ago.

He surfaced to find that he'd been staring at

her from under lowered lashes. She'd reached the point of telling him the highlights of his hotel and he raised one hand to stop her in mid-flow.

'But what about the sex angle?'

'Sex angle?'

'Don't be coy, Ms Wilson. Tell me I haven't wasted the past twenty-five minutes listening to you try and gear me up to an advertising campaign shot through a soft-focus lens?' He stood up, and suddenly the vantage point she had had standing over him was lost. 'Surely you must know what the purpose of my hotel complex is going to be?'

'I thought it might work better to highlight the stupendous surroundings and the organic nature of the buildings. In this day and age, people are very much aware of the charm of a boutique resort that is in total harmony with nature.'

She scrolled to a shot of one of the two-bedroomed villas set a short distance from the beach, just part of the package that had been emailed to her the week before by the contact she had cultivated at the resort. 'Hence the fact that all the wood used to build your hotel is locally sourced from the Caribbean.'

She flicked down to another series of artfully shot photos of the Michelin-starred cuisine that would be on offer, but she was acutely conscious of Niccolo's fabulous dark eyes resting lazily on her, with just the faintest hint of amusement.

'I've also made something of the food and the fact that much of the produce is grown on the island, with some cultivated actually in the hotel compound, and that the yoga centre is genius.'

'Yes, I've seen all the arty shots, but you're not going to win the race by showing me pictures of sunsets and palm trees. I'm not planning on enticing poets to come to my resort, to spend their time staring off into the distance admiring the scenery and then writing sonnets about it.' He raised both eyebrows sardonically and grinned. 'So, once again…is this all you've got?'

CHAPTER TWO

THE ALLOTTED HALF-HOUR timespan, which under any other circumstances Niccolo would have rigidly adhered to, was galloping fast towards its end. With his bottle of water replenished, and protein bar only just managing to take the edge off his hunger pangs, he looked at Ellie, appreciating the slow crawl of colour tingeing her cheeks.

Maybe he would be lenient and extend the stay of execution because he liked the way those big, hazel eyes were staring at him, sheepishly, faltering, yet with just an interesting hint of defiance. Also, her pitch might be ridiculously fuzzy round the edges, but the other pitches he'd seen had been way too suggestive in comparison. It wouldn't hurt to hear her out.

And she *did* have those big, hazel eyes.

This was the first time Niccolo had ever taken any interest in any of the advertising campaigns for his companies. Normally, that was left to the experts in his Sales and Marketing department.

This hotel, however, was quite separate from his business interests. This venture was solely funded from his own personal fortune. It was his baby and his alone. The excitement of running an empire was beginning to pall. *Life* was beginning to pall. He had kept his promise to his father. His duty to make sure his family was taken care of had been done, so what now? It sometimes felt as though duty was all he had been programmed to do. This hotel, and the subsequent chain of similar hotels he had in mind, had revived his jaded palate. Overseeing its development, with the select little team he had personally hand-picked, half of whom were having the time of their lives working in situ on the island, was proving to be just the tonic he needed.

And the woman sitting opposite him was having a similar effect. Very energizing.

'Of course...' Ellie broke a silence that had reached screaming point. 'I do realise that your hotel will be catering for a young, singles market...'

'Not necessarily young. In fact, I would say that young people will be in the minority. Most of them wouldn't be able to afford the prices I'm asking. But you've got the *single* part right. Single people looking for love on a holiday of a lifetime. Exquisite location, exquisite scenery—it's the ultimate place for a romantic connection to develop.

'Except all I'm seeing here is the exquisite scenery. Anyone looking at what you've put together would think that you're advertising somewhere for stars-in-their-eyes honeymooners. So, repeat, tell me what else you've got, because your competitors have all managed to hit the nail on the head with their offerings.' They hadn't, he thought, but you never showed your hand and lost the advantage. It wouldn't hurt for her to think that the competition was galloping towards the finishing line.

'I thought that it might be more tempting if guests weren't made to feel that they were there to…to…make *romantic connections.*'

Niccolo's eyebrows shot up. 'You mean, delude them into thinking that they're really there just for the blue skies and the turquoise sea—the peace and tranquillity? *Ms* Wilson, my guests will be actively seeking partners, and focusing on the scenery isn't going to tempt them, it's going to put them off.'

'If you don't like what I've done, Mr Rossi, then perhaps we shouldn't waste one another's time any longer.' But to return empty-handed was going to hurt their business. Of course, it couldn't be helped, but the agency, her career… those were the things that grounded her, that enabled her to put down roots. It represented all those steps on the ladder that would mean that she would never have to endure the insecurities she'd had to endure as a child. Her parents' wanderings had been self-imposed but Ellie knew well enough that, even if you took that out of the equation, the only way anyone could be guaranteed that their house remained their castle was to have the wherewithal to pay the mortgage.

'You're not much of a trier, are you, Ms Wilson?' Niccolo remarked dryly. 'Giving up already? Aren't you going to try to get me to see your point of view? I'm shocked that you can survive longer than two minutes in the cutthroat world of advertising where sex sells— and, the more explicit the sex, the higher the turnover of sales.' Niccolo watched the stubborn tilt of her chin with interest. 'Don't tell me you've never gone down the tawdry route of selling something stunningly dull and virtually unsaleable with the help of a few sexy images…?'

'I haven't, as it happens,' Ellie returned stiffly. She looked at his devastatingly handsome face and thought that there was little chance he would ever be able to get where she was coming from, because when you oozed sex appeal like he did it was unlikely you could ever appreciate that it wasn't just about the physical. 'The accounts I have worked on have had great success on an approach based on nostalgia, whimsy and a reminder that the good things in life don't necessarily have anything to do with sex.'

'Ah. I'm getting the picture. You're the "bread, cheese and milk" person. You leave the cars, perfume and alcohol to your more racy co-workers.' He gazed at her thoughtfully and then stood up, waiting while she scrambled hastily to her feet.

'You've already had more of my time than I'd banked on,' he told her bluntly. 'And you should have already done yourself out of a job by your charming but misdirected pitch. But here's what I'm thinking, *Ms Eleanor Wilson.* Maybe it would be unwise to fall into the trap of the obvious appeal. Needless to say, your campaign is way too hazy for my venture, but on the other hand it's not sleazy. There isn't a single saucy image, and you've managed to show me an entire pitch in which no mention is made of the fact that everyone on the complex will be looking for *a connection.* Somewhere between the "sex sells" and the romantic sunsets is what I'm looking for. So, why don't you follow me to my office and you can have the full brunt of my attention?'

He was already walking towards the door and Ellie tripped behind him, stuffing her files into the briefcase and balancing the tablet and her coat in her free hand.

Unsurprisingly, she thought sourly, the man had not offered to carry anything for her. She was grateful that she was being given a second chance to prove herself but, if he wanted to bring her round to promoting the concept of a resort where people were invited to pay a fortune so that they could hook up with similarly rich people for meaningless sex, then he was barking up the wrong tree.

Meaningless sex wasn't her thing. She could still remember the swinging parties her parents had had, the concept of free love which they had never hidden from her. Once, when she'd been eight or nine, she had burst into the kitchen for a glass of water only to find her mother wrapped round a fellow hippy houseguest. After that, she had had the talk about the birds and the bees—except, unlike most 'birds and bees' talks delivered by well-intentioned, responsible parents, hers had been liberally promoting the joys of experimental sex and the positives of being adventurous.

There was a lift that went directly from the gym, straight up to Niccolo's suite of offices on the top floor of the building. She could have been a piece of office furniture for all the attention he paid to her on the way. He worked on his phone, indolently leaning against the brushed metal panel, one hundred percent focused on whatever he was doing.

Even when the lift doors purred open, he barely raised his eyes from whatever was garnering his attention. His hair had more or less dried and he had raked his fingers through it, giving it an approximation of neatness. Gone was the raw, primal male heaving his impossible load of weights and in its place was the urbane and sophisticated billionaire who could have whatever he wanted at the click of his imperious fingers, although...

Her gaze skittered surreptitiously to him and she shivered because, suit or no suit, there was still something darkly, dangerously and thrillingly intimidating about him. She stiffened at the fanciful turn of her thoughts. She wasn't a Victorian maiden and he wasn't a swashbuckling male. She was an efficient and ambitious partner in an up-and-coming advertising agency and he was a potential client who had the capacity to put their business on the map.

She'd worked hard for this opportunity and she wasn't going to squander it.

Ellie barely noticed the plush surroundings as they disembarked on the top floor. There was a hush in the huge open space, where smoked-glass partitions and cleverly positioned plants formed barriers between some of the walnut-and-chrome desks. It was the hush of people working hard to make the billions that kept Niccolo's sprawling company at the top of the pecking order.

His offices were at the end of a thickly carpeted corridor and he only paused when he entered an outer room where a middle-aged woman was busily doing something on her computer.

'No interruptions for the next hour,' Niccolo said, sweeping past to push open his office door, then standing aside for Ellie to brush past him. 'I'll be busy.' He turned to his secretary and Ellie could detect the wicked grin in his voice. 'Ms Wilson, who's going to try and convince me that sex doesn't sell.'

Ellie knew when she was being goaded and, much as she didn't like it, discretion was the better part of valour. And who knew? Maybe she *would* be able to make him see that sex wasn't the be all and end all when it came to selling an image of fun.

'So.' Niccolo waved to one of chairs clustered around a low wooden table. His office wasn't so much one room as several rooms laid out in the manner of a very expensive, very open-plan studio apartment. There was a sitting area, a dining area and a bar area. All that was missing was a bedroom, although the deep three-seater sofa against the grey wall…

Ellie sat. The chairs were low and deep. They were designed to encourage relaxation but, since the last thing she felt was relaxed, she perched uncomfortably on the edge of one and placed her tablet on the table in front of her.

Niccolo sprawled in the chair facing her.

'You were going to try and win this contract,' he drawled, settling into the chair and loosely linking his fingers on his washboard-hard stomach. 'By showing me what you can do when *sex on the beach* meets *sunsets in paradise.*' He grinned. 'So, lose the landscaped garden appeal, and the locally sourced fruit-and-veg slideshow, and show me how you can get on board with love at first sight and adventures between the sheets.'

In that very instant, Ellie knew, without a shadow of a doubt, that there was almost no chance Niccolo was going to use her agency to promote his venture.

Her time should have been up but he found her entertaining. She could hear the thread of amusement in his voice and she could see it reflected in the lazy speculation behind his dark eyes.

He owned the company and he could do exactly what he wanted and, if he wanted to toy with her, then there was no one to stop him.

She wasn't the sort of woman he was accustomed to meeting and that was the long and short of it. He might genuinely be interested in her input, because it would be so contrary to the rest of the pitches he had heard, but in the end the job would go to the agency that fell in line with his fun-in-the-sun, hit-and-run version of love.

'I don't think I'm the right person for the job, Mr Rossi,' Ellie said politely. 'I've had a very high success rate with all the other contracts I've been given. I did truly believe that the best approach when it came to advertising your hotel would be to promote it as something classy and unique, with much more on offer than any more downmarket resorts that specifically appeal to singles, but I can see that you're not really on board with that concept.'

'How old are you?'

'I beg your pardon?'

'I'm curious because—and correct me if I'm

wrong here—you're in the service industry and yet you're allowing your own personal prejudices to get in the way. I'm finding it hard to believe that a woman in her twenties, which is what I'm assuming you are, can be so morally upright that she digs her heels in at the thought of promoting a hotel where single people can have a bit of fun in agreeable surroundings.'

Ellie met his eyes without flinching. 'I do think that romance can blossom in the sort of setting your hotel will provide, and I really do feel that that's an important aspect that should be promoted, but I just don't think I would be very good at producing an advertising campaign that focuses on people bed-hopping for two weeks.'

'You make it sound as though sex is something distasteful.' Niccolo was intrigued. She was so different from any other woman he had ever met that she could have come from another planet.

She was leaning towards him, hands gripping the sides of the chair. She had removed the frightful coat, although the jacket underneath was still firmly in place. Even so, he could still make out the white blouse and under it the shadowy silhouette of her jutting breasts.

His breathing slowed. His long lashes veiled his expression but there was a sudden stillness about him that betrayed a momentary lapse of control. The throb in his loins heralded a desire that was rock-hard and shocking because it was the last thing he'd expected. He shifted, sitting upright to try and release some of the painful pressure.

Any other woman might have tuned in to the shift in atmosphere, the crackle of electricity in the air, the tension that had settled between them, as taut as a piece of elastic pulled to breaking point.

Ms Eleanor Wilson didn't. She was staring at him with wide-eyed earnestness. She leaned forward a little further and he glimpsed the tantalising valley of her cleavage.

Niccolo abruptly reared up, his whole body on fire as be began to pace his office in an attempt to get his runaway libido back under control.

'I never said that sex was distasteful.' Ellie breathed, disconcerted by the way the conversation had veered off course and all at sea as to how she could return it to safe moorings. 'I do, however, think that a fortnight of sex isn't a recipe for sad single people finding love.'

'Why are my single guests *sad*?' Niccolo wondered what her body looked like under the granny get-up. He had always been a big fan of the woman with obvious sex appeal.

He liked to see what was on offer and, more than that, he liked knowing that the women he dated were savvy enough to know what was on the table and what wasn't. Sex was on the table and commitment wasn't.

Niccolo had made one wrong turn in his love life and, from that day on, he'd determined never to make another. Fresh out of university, and with a terminally ill family business that needed to be cobbled back together, he had looked to the girl he'd been dating for support. She'd only been on the scene for a handful of months, but she had been everything he had wanted in a woman, at that point in time.

Once the firm hand of his father had been lost, the family business had declined gracefully, like an elegant, well-bred woman ageing until she sadly became bedridden, waiting for the Grim Reaper to escort her away. It had been a gradual process that had seen the decline of their fortunes but Niccolo, even through the gradual decline, had still been privately educated and had still enjoyed the privileges of the upper-middle-class background which had given him the usual holidays abroad and, of course, the cultivated accent that Susie had claimed to adore. Darkly, sexily Italian but with the low, husky drawl of someone straight out of the upper drawer. The combination had fascinated her—had been so different from her own working-class background, which was something Niccolo had paid scant attention to.

But things had changed the minute he had divulged that the family inheritance was about to gasp its last breath. With money off the table, Susie had begun to change. It turned out that she was a lot less impressed by him than he had thought. It turned out that she had wanted the rich, young boy with a country pile and a flash apartment in Belgravia. As it turned out she very quickly found someone else who fitted the bill, someone who'd just so happened to be one of his closest friends.

Niccolo had forgiven his friend because he'd been spared a wolf in lamb's clothing.

Susie had been sexy as hell and she had known exactly what to do with her plentiful assets.

But he had never forgiven *her*. Indeed, she had come crawling to him years later, when his face was all over the press as the young lion beginning to lead the pack, and he had derived a great deal of pleasure in dispatching her—although, in truth, he could have just as easily thanked her for the lesson she had taught him. She'd focused him. She'd reminded him that love was a distraction from the obligations he had sworn to fulfil. Sex wasn't a distraction, sex was a physical release, and if he had a voracious appetite for it then he had no qualms about sating it with those willing women who weren't ashamed to pursue him. They knew the score. He always made sure of that after that youthful hiccup. His personal life was controlled as efficiently as his public one.

When it came to women, Niccolo *always* knew what he was getting into.

'I never said that your guests were *sad,*' Ellie said, fervent and sincere. 'But I do think that love isn't something that can be manufactured by throwing people together for a couple of weeks. Love is something that takes time. You're selling no-strings-attached sex and I... I...'

'Don't approve?' Niccolo interjected helpfully. 'Some might say that I'm doing a service for a certain sector of society who find it difficult to join the dating pool. No, wait, that's not quite right—they find it very easy to join the dating pool. The only problem is that the pool is often full of sharks and piranha. My clients are in search of more tranquil waters.'

'I'm not following you.'

'The other agencies I interviewed—and you were lucky to be considered because I only interviewed a total of three—offered me precisely what they imagined was written on the can. A singles resort for people to meet one another. Sex on the beach, but in a more glamorous than average setting, and with the protagonists wearing expensive swim wear and designer sunglasses. I got the impression that they were advertising the sort of place they would personally find appealing themselves.'

'I thought you wanted the obvious approach.'

'I said I didn't want a selection of tasteful shots of the seasonal menus on offer.' He looked at her thoughtfully. 'Tell me what landing this job would mean to you,' he murmured. 'You clearly have talent, likewise ambition, and you're good at what you do. I've done my homework. It's a small job, but it's for me, and that in itself makes it a small but extremely worthwhile job. Am I right?'

Ellie looked down at her linked fingers. What he had just said was boldly, offensively arrogant but it had been said with such nonchalant self-assurance that she could only find herself meekly agreeing with his summary of the situation.

It was a small job in terms of exposure but huge in terms of possibilities. Which was why it had been so fabulous that their agency had been invited to pitch for it.

'I see you get where I'm going with his. So tell me what it would mean to you, personally, if this job were to go to your agency. And I don't want to hear any company spiel about your small but upwardly mobile business and how well you connect with the youth of today.'

'Why does it matter what it would mean to me?'

Niccolo took his time in answering. She was in an office, he was in his suit. He could tell that thankfully the natural order of things had been restored. This was her comfort zone and she was in charge of the brief she was sworn to deliver.

'Let's just say that I'm curious and, since I'm the one with the chequebook, why don't you humour me?'

'For obvious reasons,' Ellie said stiffly, 'This would be a wonderful feather in my cap, and certainly cement my place as on a par with my partners who have both had more experience than myself. As you rightly said, it may not be the biggest of commissions, but you're a big cheese, so there's always the hope that other significant commissions might follow. It would be a brilliant CV builder for the agency and an even greater one for me.'

Niccolo's eyebrows winged up. 'The way you said *big cheese* doesn't make it sound like a compliment. So, you get this job and you further prove yourself...'

'Yes,' Ellie told him flatly.

'And your career means a great deal to you.'

'It means everything to me.' She met his dark gaze and held it. 'Financial independence means everything to me. This job offers me a door through which the agency can enter and I want to see what's on the other side of that door. So, *that's* how much it means to me.'

Niccolo frowned, momentarily distracted. 'What about all the usual things women your age busy themselves thinking about?' He was astonished at how sexist he sounded, because he prided himself on providing equal opportunities for women, and was known for parity on every level when it came to hiring within his own companies. For heaven's sake, he'd gone into this venture on the back of what one of his sisters had said in passing because he'd respected her opinion even though it didn't happen to coincide with his.

'I'm not following you, Mr Rossi.'

'Marriage and children? You're clearly ultra-conservative, but that doesn't seem to tie in with the *I'll do anything for my career* angle.'

'I'm very focused on my career right now, Mr Rossi. I don't have time for the sort of relationship that would lead to marriage and children.'

'Interesting approach.'

'Why interesting?'

'You meet someone.' Niccolo was fascinated by her approach, which roughly mirrored his. 'And you discover you want a relationship because something is ignited. I didn't think women spent much time working out how they could fit it into their work schedule but, forgive me, I'm digressing.'

When was the last time he'd done that?

'What I am really interested in is finding out how flexible your schedule is and whether there is anyone on the scene who might impact on your flexibility or any urgent work commitments that cannot be temporarily diverted.'

'I just don't understand what you're asking, Mr Rossi...'

'I like what you've done, Ms Wilson. It may need a little tweaking, but the more I think about it the more I accept that there's something to be said for the fading sunset shots. They're tasteful. I can understand why you're probably the queen of whimsy in your company. Unfortunately, you've brought personal issues to the table, and I'm getting the impression that because you disapprove of the concept of my hotel you would find it difficult to work in any changes that might be necessary.'

'It's my job to adapt to and interpret what

the client wants,' Ellie said, brain going over-time to work out where this was going.

'Splendid reply!'

'But what does that have to do with whether there's anyone in my life who can impact on my job or whether I have other jobs on the go?' Ellie looked at him with a perplexed frown.

'I'm prepared to give your company a shot at this,' Niccolo told her.

'That's wonderful! Although…' She frowned. 'You still haven't answered my question.' She hesitated, wishing she could read what was going through his head behind those deep, dark, shuttered eyes that were looking at her with the sort of lazy assessment that could make a per-son feel drugged and heavy-limbed. 'And…' She inhaled deeply. 'I'm curious as to *why* you've decided to give us the job.'

'Because you have backbone,' Niccolo ob-served, enjoying the transparency of her face. 'You happen to be off-target about my resort—and I can personally guarantee that all of my guests would be very much affronted at being written off as *sad*—but you didn't allow me to cow you into saying what you thought I might want to hear.'

Ellie flushed with pleasure even though there was a lot to sift through in what he just said before she could reach the compliment.

'I expect,' she conceded, 'That you must have that effect on people. They put themselves out to please you.'

Niccolo didn't bother denying it.

'The reason I asked you whether there was anyone in your life and whether you could be spared at work is because I feel that you might need convincing, first hand, of the product you'll be commissioned to advertise. Put it this way—it's no good trying to sell a bar of chocolate if you don't like the stuff. How could the message possibly be sincere?'

'Need convincing?' Ellie wondered how Niccolo Rossi imagined that he could try and talk her into dumping her moral code. Did he think that people's ingrained beliefs were interchangeable depending on the time of day? Or maybe he thought that he was so persuasive that it didn't matter *what* someone believed in—if it didn't happen to coincide with his beliefs, then he would be able to win them over because he was a smooth talker. Or just too plain sexy for his own good.

Her eyes drifted to the sensual curve of his mouth and she hurriedly looked away and mentally gathered her wits.

'I don't have to be convinced of anything to do a good job. I'm grateful for the opportunity to prove to you just what I can come up with. I think I'm getting an idea of what you want, and I want to reassure you that I will be able to deliver. I'm assuming that you have a deadline? I gather that the resort is due to open imminently. I assure you I will have no problem working to any deadline you care to set.'

'I'm thrilled to hear that,' Niccolo said dryly. 'But, before you get too excited talking deadlines and delivery schedules, I feel we should sort out any potential crossed wires here.' His dark eyes rested on her face with just a whisper of sardonic amusement. 'I'm not asking you to make another appointment with my secretary for a follow-up meeting in a week's time. I'm asking you to pay a little visit to my resort, see for yourself what it's all about.' Niccolo seldom did anything purely on impulse. This was impulsive.

He took a few seconds to savour the rare sensation of a woman clearly appalled at the prospect of having to endure time out in a six-star luxury resort, all expenses paid.

'So, do you want the job? Then pack your bags, Ms Wilson.' He smiled lazily, 'I've been told that nothing beats a spot of winter sun...'

CHAPTER THREE

NICCOLO HADN'T KNOWN, until a handful of hours before his private jet was due to take off, whether he would give in to yet more impulsive behaviour and take time out to go to the Caribbean.

His timetable was locked down tighter than a bank vault. He had meetings upon meetings, all meticulously planned weeks in advance. He had conference calls scheduled for ungodly hours of the morning, because it was imperative to be able to connect with clients on the other side of the world. His social life had been reduced to three business events, none of which could be avoided.

There was no way he could play truant because a random woman had shown up in his gym a week ago and done something to his rigid self-control.

Yes, he'd told her that going to his resort would be part of the job. So far, so good, because that made perfect sense. He'd liked the fact that she hadn't been intimidated by him into agreeing to submit what the other advertising companies had submitted. He'd admired the way she'd dug her heels in, even though he had disagreed with pretty much everything she had had to say about relationships.

And yes, he had, sitting opposite her, been tempted by a number of *what if?* scenarios.

But even as he'd been tempted, even as he'd acknowledged the weird, disconcerting impact she seemed to have on his nether regions, a part of him had remained contained, controlled and logical.

He wasn't going to go there because it didn't make sense. He'd enjoyed the brief lapse of control, and had had fun playing around with images in his head, but deep down he had fully expected to relegate her to the back of his mind the second she left his office.

Face it, he was used to dating queens of the catwalk and, even though Ms Eleanor Wilson had a certain undeniable something that made him frown and want to take a second look, she was no queen of the catwalk. No jutting cheekbones, no sinewy arms, no legs up to armpits. Average, really, and with a dress sense that would have had *fashionistas* screaming in horror and running for the hills.

But, for some ungodly reason, the woman had lodged in his head like a burr and he couldn't understand it.

He did, however, know himself and he knew, without a shadow of a doubt, that he needed to see her again because he wasn't prepared for the tedium of having her in his system.

His relationship with the opposite sex bordered on the ridiculously predictable. He either had a business relationship with them, in which case they had about as much sex appeal as a potted plant in a suit, or else he had a sexual relationship with them, in which case they played the usual games of seduction before the whole thing became stale and he moved on.

He knew where he stood with women and he liked it that way. Despite his mother's disapproval, and his sisters' tiresome nagging, he was very happy indeed with his love life because it held no unfortunate surprises.

He'd endured one of those and, as far as he was concerned, one learning curve was enough for a lifetime.

Ms Eleanor Wilson, however, had managed uncomfortably to straddle both areas, which was why he'd found himself thinking about her way too often for his liking.

Which was why he knew that he had to see her again, if only to prove to himself that whatever appeal she had exercised was all in his mind.

Niccolo told himself that his baffling attraction to the woman was not, however, sufficient draw to take him away from his duties back in London. Truthfully, he knew that he could do with seeing where his money was going, and touching base with the people out there spending it on his behalf. He had paid a flying visit to the place months before, at which point he had put in place everything he wanted, and thereafter the whole show had been left in the capable hands of the small team of people who were employed by him exclusively to handle the project.

He had been updated daily with progress reports. He knew exactly what was going on but emails and conference calls were a poor substitute for face-to-face inspection. If Ms Eleanor Wilson was out there as well, then her presence would certainly add a tantalising piquancy to the trip. But first and foremost, he reasoned, this was about business, and if it was a little unexpected it was no more than a trip he would have done anyway, if at a slightly later date. At any rate, money was money, and he would be interested to see what she made of the resort because that would determine how genuine her ad campaign would eventually be and, if she wasn't up to scratch, then regrettably she would have to go. Nothing was signed and he was well aware that she knew the implications of that. She had drawn even with the field but hadn't yet cleared the finishing line.

He was musing over this when he spotted her approaching, dragging a small case behind her and with a capacious bag that could have housed a kitchen sink slung over her shoulder.

Immediately, he stilled and, eyes narrowed, he watched as she walked towards him.

'Is that it?' he asked, eyeing the tiny suitcase, which was hardly bigger than a rucksack. 'You *were* allowed as much luggage as you wanted.'

Hot and bothered and feeling out of her depth, Ellie wondered whether that question required a reply. She'd had no idea who would be accompanying her on the flight over to the island and had, at first, assumed that there might also be other candidates being taken there on probation. She had been contacted by his secretary and informed of all the necessary details for a seven-day stay on the island. She had come close to looking forward to the working break until, in the chauffeurdriven car that had been dispatched for her, she'd received a call from Niccolo's very nice secretary who had cheerfully informed her that

Niccolo himself would be meeting her at the airport.

'But he can't be!' Ellie had had to stop herself from wailing in despair. 'How can he spare the time? He could barely spare the time to keep his appointment with me!'

'Mr Rossi can do as he likes,' his secretary had said gently. 'He's a law unto himself.'

Horror had kicked in fast and the remainder of the drive had been spent in a state of nervous tension because, ever since her unconventional meeting with the man who was a law unto himself, Ellie had had to fight giving in to the insidious temptation to waste time thinking about him. He had quizzed her, and questioned her, and challenged her, and since when was all that part of the job? He was rich and good-looking, so felt that he could do as he pleased even though he had known well enough that she had been unsettled by the way he had overstepped her boundaries.

Ellie could have told him that she had no intention of changing her beliefs or suddenly turning into someone who approved of casual sex just because she happened to be being considered for an advertising campaign promoting it.

However, this was not just any client, and she had been prepared to factor in Niccolo

Rossi's unorthodox approach. She had told herself that, left to her own devices on the island, she would relax and tailor her approach to better suit what he required. She had been buoyed by the fact that, despite his initial criticisms, he had been more swayed by her tasteful take than what her competitors had put on the table. She would take that edge and work with it.

Everything changed the second she found out that Niccolo was going to be accompanying her.

'Allow me to help you with the case,' he murmured politely, leading the way through a series of unfamiliar turns and twists until they were finally on a separate landing strip where, poised like a giant black-and-silver bird of prey, stood his private jet. 'I hope you've packed enough...' Dark eyes slid over to her. She was certainly making sure that she didn't get into the holiday spirit, he observed. What she was wearing was identical to what she had been wearing the last time they'd met, except for the colour. This nightmare was a silvery shade of grey. Her hair was as severely tied back now as it had been then, and she was currently averting her eyes, just as she had been for most of the time she had been in his presence.

Which said something.

He felt a charge of adrenaline rush through

his system. She was so…*incredibly prissy*. Right now, she was striding forcefully alongside him, but he could sense nervous tension, and the unwitting combination stirred something reckless and wicked inside him.

'You look a little tense, Ms Wilson. Eleanor. Shall we move onto a first-name basis, bearing in mind that we'll be spending the next few days in one another's company?'

'I'm not tense.' She pretended not to see his outstretched hand, raised to usher her onto the first of the metal steps up to the plane. 'I'm incredibly relaxed, as a matter of fact.' She gripped the rails to move ahead of him and was then instantly conscious of the fact that he was now behind her, probably eyeing up her uninspiring figure and her even more uninspiring choice of clothes.

But she was here for work, and work was going to remain uppermost in her mind. Even when she'd thought that she would be travelling solo, or else with one of his many minions, or even with other contenders for the job, she had not been tempted to go frothy or frilly with her outfit for the flight over.

For a start, she didn't own anything frothy or frilly, so that took care of that.

'You were going to tell me why you're travelling so light.' Niccolo followed her into his jet. He wondered how his libido could suddenly become so inconveniently active in the presence of someone who was so buttoned up, both physically and mentally. But then, the second he started thinking about buttons, he began to think about the pleasure he could have undoing them, at which point he decided that the safest option would be to work for the hours they would be spending in the air.

'Was I?' Ellie barely heard him because she was so awed by her surroundings.

She'd travelled a lot in her time but her memories of planes had been of being scrunched in the back between her parents, desperately trying to pretend that they were just a little less outlandish in their dress, just a little more *normal*.

Since those heady days of being toted all over the globe like an accessory, her only trips had been within the United Kingdom on business and rarely involving a stop over.

She'd never flown business class and certainly not first. And *certainly* had never contemplated getting on a private jet. Had never wondered what it might be like. Now she felt she could safely say that it exceeded all expectations.

From the cream leather seats and the walnut trims, to the unusual layout that catered for sleep and work, to the smiling staff ready and waiting to make sure that every whim was met at the fastest possible speed.

From the champagne to greet them, which Ellie politely declined, to the offer of pyjamas, which so horrified her that she was left almost speechless and could barely splutter out another polite refusal.

'Surely you will want to get into something a little more comfortable, Eleanor?' Niccolo murmured just as soon as they were seat in chairs as big as sofa beds.

'Ellie,' she corrected because 'Eleanor' was sending little shivers racing up and down her spine.

'Ellie.' His smile was sinfully attractive and, from his lips, the word 'Ellie' managed to send the same shivers racing through her. 'It's a long flight.'

'No, thank you. I'll be fine.' She cracked a smile. He, of course, looked impossibly sexy in a pair of faded black jeans and a long-sleeved black, stretchy tee shirt that fitted him as snugly as a glove. Granted it was his jet, and he could have shown up barefoot and wearing a bin bag, but she got the impression that he was so sure of himself that, even if he had been travelling first class on a commercial jet, he would still have worn exactly what he was wearing now.

'Well,' He shrugged. 'The offer's there.'

'Do many people who use this plane slip into pyjamas when they're travelling?' Ellie asked a little tartly and Niccolo grinned.

'I have no idea. I either travel alone or else I'm with…a companion. And slipping into pyjamas isn't usually an option because they generally don't show up wearing suits and high-heeled shoes.'

A flash of white teeth and an amused smile left Ellie in no doubt that the companions in question were of the female variety and not there to discuss work related issues.

'I must say,' Ellie confessed, 'That I'm surprised that you're coming on this trip. I thought that you might have been too busy to spare the time. Will you…er…be staying for the full seven days? Because I just want to reassure you that there's no need at all for you to think that you have to hold my hand just in case I'm out of my depth. I shall be perfectly happy to explore on my own and work what I observe into new material.'

'Anyone would think that you didn't want me around.'

'Not at all! I just wouldn't want to put you out. But,' she hazarded hopefully, 'I'm guessing that you'll have lots of other things to be getting on with out there?'

'Undoubtedly. This is a perfect opportunity for me to check on my little venture—make sure that all the nuts and bolts are in place. In fact, the first flurry of guests have already touched down. I feel it's only good manners to introduce myself to them, although it has to be said that my team out there are superb.'

Ellie relaxed. If he was going to be busy checking nuts and bolts and entertaining his guests, then he wasn't going to have much time to shadow her, a prospect she found unnerving to say the least.

'That said,' Niccolo drawled, 'I wouldn't want you to feel neglected. No, let me finish! You stand a far better chance of delivering what I want if I'm right there showing you first-hand the experience the guests in my hotel are subscribing to.'

'Is there someone there who acts as matchmaker?' Ellie asked as she tried to fathom exactly what variation of *experience* Niccolo could be referring to, when the only one on offer was casual sex if two people just so happened to be attracted to one another physically.

'No,' he said kindly. 'This isn't a dating agency. It's a venue for meeting like-minded souls.'

'Like-minded souls.'

'The world can be a perilous place,' Niccolo said coolly, 'when a man or a woman with money puts themselves out there in search of a relationship. Gold-diggers come in all shapes and sizes and ending up having to deal with one is an experience most people would want to avoid. I'm setting the scene where, at least, some of the uncertainty can be removed.' He shrugged. 'I don't promise that the people who come to my resort shouldn't still be cautious. There's only so much one can do.'

'Do you speak from experience?' Ellie heard herself say, question asked before she had time to take it back. Dark eyes met her hazel ones and this time there was no easy charm just a cool, cool warning.

'You're not here to try and delve into my personal life,' Niccolo intoned, his rich, dark voice threaded with just a hint of a warning.

'I'm sorry. I wasn't asking...'

'Yes, Ellie, you were. My personal life is out of bounds.'

'Yet you seem happy to quiz me about mine,' Ellie pointed out, barely aware that the plane had long since taken off and the journey across the Atlantic had begun.

'Have I done that?'

'You've criticised me for being traditional in my outlook.'

'I haven't criticised you. I've been bemused,

because it's not often I come into contact with a woman who turns her nose up at a relationship that doesn't have an engagement ring at the end of it. That's not criticism, Ellie. That's known as voicing an opinion. Were I to quiz you about your personal life, then, trust me, you would know about it.'

Ellie didn't say anything but chose to give him a defiant, fulminating look from under her lashes. She felt all hot under the collar and the sensible outfit that she had chosen to travel in was already beginning to chafe at her skin.

The way he was staring at her, as if mentally working her out so that he could store the information in his computer banks, wasn't helping either.

She ran a slender finger round the collar of her shirt and surreptitiously undid a button so that she could get some air to her heated skin.

Niccolo knew when to leave well alone. Now was that time. Unfortunately, he had no intention of paying attention to common sense, because for the first time in as long as he could remember he was enjoying himself. He'd expected his memories of her to have been fanciful and skewed. He had quickly discovered that they were neither.

In the wings, one of the two members of his crew who took care of the jet was waiting on standby in case anything was needed. He beckoned her across with just the merest of signals and on cue she delivered two glasses of champagne to them, along with a platter of delicious snacks which she placed on the table between them.

'A sip of alcohol won't hurt,' he urged, handing her the glass. 'It'll relax you.'

'As I said, I'm extremely relaxed,' Ellie told him tightly, but she took the glass and sure enough, after a couple of mouthfuls, she felt a little less strung out.

'That's better! Now that we both understand that all matters of a personal nature are off the table, I've got a stack of work to get through, so I'll leave you to your own devices. There's ample food on board, including hot food, so give me a shout when you're hungry.' He thought for a bit. 'Although, you'll probably feel embarrassed to put your hand up and ask to be fed, so I'll get one of the crew to bring something round in a couple of hours, and if you're asleep or you're not hungry then you can always send him on his way. How about that?'

Ellie's skin prickled all over. He was so assured, so smooth, so urbane and sophisticated, that she felt gauche and awkward in his presence. She didn't know how to deal with a layer of charm and charisma that was in a league of its own.

He had zoomed in and made assumptions about something that struck at the very core of her because, for all that she was focused on her career, and no matter that it was a goal in which she firmly believed, she truly did sometimes wonder whether life wasn't passing her by.

She had compiled so many check-lists for the perfect guy—the guy who would be as grounded as she was, as uninterested in wandering the world, as focused on stability—that no one yet had come close to getting past the starting gate.

Her dream of the little house where she would be able to put down roots, roots that could never, ever be yanked up, with a man who would never grow bored with the joys of the ordinary, was in danger of becoming lost under the weight of her self-imposed restrictions.

Ellie had been out with several men over the years but none of those men had worked out, and it was frustrating, because they had all ticked the right boxes. Two had been teachers, as industrious and as caring as anyone could get, and the third had been a solicitor. They'd all fitted the bill and yet none of them had been *quite right.* The last time she had visited her parents, her mother had pulled her to one side and asked her, in that forthright manner she had always had, where the boyfriends were. Then, having given her a long talk about them *not minding at all* if her sexual interests *lay in another direction,* she had come right out and told her that, all things being equal, she was probably too fussy.

Ellie had nearly burst out laughing. Too fussy? She had spent too many years observing the behaviour of men and women who weren't fussy, and she'd take fussy any day of the week, thank you very much!

Although, her bed *was* still cold and empty, and every so often she caught herself wondering whether *she* wasn't the one with the problem. Was she frigid? Surely, by now, *someone* should have ignited a spark, stirred her imagination, made her daydream?

Ellie had made herself stop thinking about the inadequacies of her personal life, and asking herself what was wrong with her—but now, with one stupid, flippant sentence, Niccolo Rossi had opened the door behind which her disappointment had been quietly hidden, and she hated him for doing that.

'You're right,' she said coldly. 'Let's make a pact right now to steer clear of any personal questions. It's not part of my brief to answer any.'

Niccolo gave her a long, measured look. She was putting up a *'No Trespassing'* sign. Didn't she know that there was nothing more tempting than a *'No Trespassing'* sign? Especially for a man like him who enjoyed the thrill of a challenge. A man for whom challenges had become pretty thin on the ground of late.

'As long as you're willing to make a pact to be open-minded about my resort.'

'That won't be happening,' Ellie told him bluntly. 'But I can assure you that my personal beliefs will not affect the end result I'll be able to show you.'

'You need to stop *assuring* me of things. It bores me when you slide into agency talk.'

Ellie reddened and looked at him with helpless frustration. She was close enough to see the lines at the corners of his eyes, to appreciate the ridiculous length of his lashes, to feel that awful, confusing 'sinking in quicksand' sensation she seemed to get when she was in his presence.

He was so unlike any man she had ever met before. Seductively easy to talk to, he was the sort of person she suspected could sell ice to Eskimos but wouldn't bother unless there was something in it for him. He was so successful that the ruthless edge would be there, underneath the lazy charm, but he was good at hiding that ruthless edge. She felt that he probably only brought it out when necessary. He was a man who got exactly what he wanted and, if the straightforward route there was blocked, he would never give up. He would just find a different way through.

And he was so unfairly gorgeous.

'I wouldn't dream of boring you.' She sucked in a breath, then gathered herself, but it took effort. 'In fact, you have to tell me the second I start doing that.' She flashed him a bright, wide smile. 'My job is to get you excited about my campaign. If I'm boring you, then I'm not doing my job properly.'

Niccolo didn't say anything. The more she traipsed back to her job, the more he wanted to yank her away from it.

She looked about as relaxed as a plank of wood although her hair was beginning to break free of its confines. He wondered what she did for fun. She seemed so uptight. Did she ever have fun? Was fun allowed in her upward career climb? He'd never met any woman who didn't have fun at the top of her agenda, especially when the woman happened to be in his company.

An errant thought flitted through his head and then out of it before he could pin it down.

This was the sort of woman his mother would approve of—the sort of woman who didn't sell her story to a cheap tabloid, the sort of woman who didn't think that the world began and ended with a well-stocked designer wardrobe and a flashy sports car.

Niccolo almost laughed out loud, because experience had taught him that there was no such thing as a safe bet when it came to women, and because one woman's head could be turned by expensive jewellery and a flashy car didn't mean that she was any less honourable than the woman who set her sights in a different direction.

Chances were high that they were equally dishonourable.

Which didn't mean you couldn't have fun with them. You just had to know when the fun was in danger of overstaying its welcome, and he was an expert when it came to that. Which might have led to the occasional awkward kiss-and-tell story but better that than leading a woman into thinking there might be more on the table.

'Fair enough,' he murmured, non-committal. 'Now, I'm going to work. Don't forget to ask for whatever you want and, if you *do* start to feel a tad uncomfortable in your office gear, the offer of something less starchy is there.' He grinned and eyed her office gear with a leisurely appraisal that set Ellie's teeth on edge.

Dismissed, she turned to the book she had brought with her. She was dreading the next few days, yet she couldn't suppress a certain feeling of excitement, which she did her utmost to ignore.

If it bothered her that a fantastic and unexpected trip to the tropics made her anxious, which any other human being would have been looking forward to, then she grounded herself by focusing on the goals she had set herself over the years. Sensible goals. That was what mattered and, if Niccolo Rossi did weird things to her that she found unsettling, then she would have to find a way of dealing with it.

She refused to beat herself up over her reaction to him. He was going to be around for the next week and then, after that, they would both return to their normal routine and she probably wouldn't see him again, unless by some miracle her agency did win the contract. This trip into unknown territory would be worth it if the deal was sealed and the job came to them.

She knew herself and she knew that, whatever he stirred up in her, it was because she was inexperienced and he was dangerously experienced. He wouldn't even be aware of her reaction to him because his spellbinding magnetism and heady, mesmerising charisma formed part of his personality, and he would only notice a woman's response if he was deliberately targeting her to get her into bed. Ellie didn't know how she knew that. *She just did.*

Knowledge was power, though, and it soothed her to think that she had analysed the situation and was therefore protected from any fallout.

She would shut down any hint of personal conversation. It would be easy, because they would be surrounded by people, and, however much he threatened to hold her hand and walk her through the process of trying to get her to get with the programme and dump all her principles, he would be busy dealing with all the teething problems of his brand-new project. He wouldn't have *time* to be annoying.

She would be safe from his flirting, which he wasn't even aware he was doing!

Because she was the last person in the world a man like that would ever consciously flirt with.

Relieved to have everything back in perspective, Ellie closed her eyes and wasn't even aware of the flight until she was shaken awake and told that they were due to land.

CHAPTER FOUR

ELLIE KNEW WHAT the resort looked like because she had been sent copies of some of the promotional shots. A low, tasteful villa housed the main administration area in addition to various bars and restaurants, and two infinity swimming pools that were serviced by separate bars. The guests stayed in individual villas. The most basic, judging from the pictures, still screamed 'luxury'.

What she *hadn't* banked on was the explosive heat that greeted them as they went from jet to SUV. It was a barrier that visibly pulsed and her clothes immediately reacted by clinging to her like glue.

'It's beautiful here.' She managed to make some small talk as they were whisked off for the short ride to the resort. She fanned herself with one hand, very much aware that she would be looking far from her best because she was perspiring from every pore

'I picked the island because it's sparsely populated,' Niccolo commented, sprawling against the door of the car and swivelling his big body so that he was looking at her. 'There's a main airport, which can handle smaller planes that fly in from some of the bigger islands, but the airstrip here is big enough for a private jet, which is the form of transport that will probably be used by a lot of the paying guests.'

'I had no idea there were that many rich people who couldn't manage to find themselves a date without the help of an outside party.'

Niccolo smiled lazily, taking no offence. 'How many wealthy people do you meet on a daily basis?' he offered smoothly.

'Not a lot,' she admitted.

'Which would explain why you can't see the grey areas. In your mind, people who have money should find it easy to locate anyone they want, but many wealthy people are intensely private and very cautious. A lot of the men are strangely shy, particularly those who have made their fortunes in areas away from the public arena. We live in a world of dotcom billionaires. For some of those billionaires, chatting up women *or* men doesn't come easy.'

'But isn't it going to be just as difficult chatting up prospective partners wherever they happen to be?'

'Good question. No.' He dealt her a slashing smile and caught her eye. 'There will be the distraction of activities—snorkelling and all sorts of other water sports. The scenery on the island is amazing—densely forested in some areas with quite remarkable bird life. They may find that they net a bird in their hand while watching a couple in the bush.'

Undermined by his wit, Ellie raised her eyebrows and said with saccharine sweetness, 'I thought you were aiming to avoid sleazy.'

Niccolo burst out laughing. 'Omit that line in your campaign,' he advised, and then, before he could take her down any more treacherous routes, he began chatting to her about the island, filling her in about the attractions to be found despite its relative size and isolation.

In a few short sentences, he built a more complete picture of the place in her head than any number of promotional shots could have done.

He pointed out a thousand different species of plants and flowers, until she said with a hint of grudging admiration, 'You seem to know an awful lot about the area.'

'I'm a man who believes in doing my homework,' he returned. 'Are you surprised? Did you think I was the sort who would dump money into setting up a resort on an island like this without first getting to know the place and the people so that I could construct something as best suited to their needs as possible?'

'I do realise that the eco-credentials are brilliant.' Ellie flushed because, frankly, he wasn't too far from the truth in what he had said and she knew that he was well aware of that from the thoughtful way he was staring at her, which made her flush even more.

'That's what I mean about revisiting those hard and fast rules of yours, Ellie,' he said, voice silky-soft but still managing to make her squirm. 'You think one thing and then you seem to cling to it like a drowning man clinging to a life belt.'

'I'm certainly prepared to concede that I hadn't expected you to be as much in the loop as you are, right down to being able to tell me what the local fauna and flora consist of,' she said firmly, avoiding the wicked gleam in his eyes. He could have been a lawyer, she thought. He seemed to have mastered the art of tying a person up in knots. Or maybe it was just her.

She tore her gaze away from him and only realised that they were already approaching the extensive grounds of his resort because the vehicle was slowing slightly. In the distance the strip of blue sea lay to the left, glimpsed be-

tween the ramrod-straight, slender trunks of
the palm trees. To the right, the mountains rose
up, thick and dense with bamboo trees and all
the various species Niccolo had impressively
listed moments before.

The car swept through a towering cathedral
of bamboo trees and then the resort was in
front of them, far, far more stunning, bathed
in the early evening sunshine, than any photo
could possibly have conveyed.

'Wow.' Ellie's eyes rounded and she leant
forward, not wanting to miss a second of the
spectacular vision in front of her.

The hotel and surrounding villas occupied
acres of land, yet it felt as though none of the
palm trees or any of the colourful plants had
been cleared to make way for the resort. Everything seemed to be dotted to accommodate
the lay of the land. The main building, she
saw as they neared it, was staggered around
the trees, yielding to them. In between, Ellie
glimpsed villas nestled like tiny jewels here
and there. Between some of the trees, there
were benches that looked as though they'd
been hewn from the ground, and hammocks
strung between tree trunks.

'Glad you came?' Niccolo asked softly, so
that her attention was dragged back to him
and she found that he was looking at her as if

he could read every thought flitting through her head.

He leaned across without warning to open her door for her and she pulled back sharply, breath indrawn as his arm brushed against her breasts.

'I don't bite,' he laughed, eyebrows raised. 'At least,' he couldn't help adding, because he knew how she would react, 'not unless I'm invited to.'

'Very funny,' Ellie muttered, bright red. 'I'm sure you find it hilarious to try and embarrass me. Are you like that with everyone you work with?'

'No,' Niccolo told her thoughtfully.

'Then why are you like that with me?' Her heart was beating hard and fast behind her ribcage. The heat pouring into the air-conditioned car was nothing next to the heat surging through her body. Niccolo's dark eyes resting on her face were doing all sorts of crazy things to her.

Ellie thought that this was what it felt like to be playing with fire, and playing with fire was something she had never done in her life before.

For one crazy moment, she actually thought that he was going to lean towards her and kiss her then, just like that, her imagination took flight and she wondered what that would be like. What would his mouth feel like on hers? Exploring her? Teasing her with his tongue? He'd be a great kisser.

The heat coursing through her veins settled between her legs. The unbridled lust which had eluded her all her adult life now assaulted her like a robber in the night.

Horrified, Ellie blinked, desperate to clear the effect that handsome, lean face and those deep, deep eyes were having on her.

'Don't answer that,' she said quickly, looking away to push open the car door and break the electric connection that was wreaking havoc with her composure. She glanced over her shoulder. 'But I'm here to work.'

'Of course you are,' Niccolo soothed. 'And my apologies if I am proving to be a distraction you're finding difficult to cope with.'

'Don't be ridiculous. You're not a distraction.'

'Then why are you acting like a cat on a hot tin roof?'

'I'm not,' Ellie denied flatly and, before he could carry on the conversation and suck her further into depths she had no intention of exploring, she leapt out of the car and stood for a few moments to get her bearing.

'First impressions?'

Ellie shifted and then looked up at him, shading her eyes, although in the space of half an hour the evening had already begun to draw in. 'It's stunning. The pictures I saw didn't do it justice. When do the first guests start arriving?'

'Quite a few are already here' Niccolo began walking briskly in the direction of a bank of palm trees and Ellie tripped behind him. 'They're probably resting in their villas. Everything here starts early and ends early. It's a consequence of the heat.'

'What about…er…?'

'What about…er…what?' Niccolo looked down at her. 'You're going to have to help me out here. At least until my mind-reading classes have been completed.'

'I *thought* that perhaps there would have been more of a night life…'

'Ah. Funny. I thought that was what you were going to say. Maybe I don't need those mind-reading classes after all.' He spun round and carried on walking, swerving left over a dwarf bridge. Ahead of them was one of the main hotel areas, flawlessly modern inside and accessed through glass doors so that none of the cool air escaped.

For a while, the conversation was halted as Niccolo did the rounds, chatting with various employees, introducing her in passing, asking a host of technical questions that alerted her to the fact that, although he had probably only been to the resort rarely, he was still on top of everything going on inside it, right down to what work remained to be done and why.

The employees were all polished and welcoming. The advertiser in Ellie was already forming impressions that would be reflected in any new directions her pitch would take and already she could understand why Niccolo had made the decision to bring her to the resort.

Through the open-plan foyer, Ellie could see some of the guests relaxing in a comfortable, spacious area that was dotted with tables and chairs that could be arranged to suit. There were plants here and there, and an enormous overhead fan that was largely unnecessary, given that the room was air-conditioned, but completed the picture of exquisite, laid-back luxury.

They didn't go there, although she could see Niccolo's sharp eyes taking it all in, making sure that everything met his high standards.

He oozed power, a man who knew exactly where he was going and how he was going to get here.

She would be an idiot to be fooled by his easy charm into thinking he was actually like everyone else. He wasn't. He simply concealed his ruthlessness well. He didn't throw his weight around—he didn't wield a whip or insist that people bow down before him because he was wealthy and powerful. He didn't have to. He had a far more successful method of ensuring the world did as he wanted.

He used the massive persuasive force of his personality. Ellie had seen the way everyone had jumped to attention around him. Not because they were intimidated, but because they were desperate to please him.

Instinctively, she sensed that that seductive persuasiveness could be far more lethal than cold arrogance or an open ability to instil fear.

She found that he had led her to a bar and restaurant area. It was small, intimate, and again he greeted the man serving behind the gleaming wooden counter with a familiarity that surprised her.

'Do you know *everyone* here on a first name basis?' she asked with genuine curiosity once they were sitting in front of a couple of long, cold fruit drinks.

'I've always found that it pays to take a healthy interest in the people who work for you.' Niccolo settled back in his chair and looked at her with the same assessing expression she found so unsettling. 'It's the safest way to avoid unpleasant surprises,' he murmured, draining the remainder of his drink, and then, without having to signal to the waiter, somehow managing to convey that he now wanted a beer. 'Plus,' he added, 'If you're liked as well as respected, you get complete and unswerving loyalty. In my line of work, I've met many a tyrant who rules through fear. They're usually the ones who find themselves manning a deserted ship the second the waters get a little choppy because all the deck hands have abandoned their posts.'

Iron fist in a velvet glove, Ellie thought with a little shiver. And yet, still so unfairly compelling.

'We were talking about the wild night-life you expected to find.' Niccolo brought her back to the present.

'Yes,' Ellie admitted. 'I assumed that there would be stuff laid on for your guests, bearing in mind that they're here to…to…meet people.'

'Like I said, this is all about keeping everything low key. Besides, I can't imagine my guests would be interested in spending an evening of karaoke.'

'Karaoke can be fun!' Ellie objected and Niccolo laughed, a deep, velvety laugh that made her tummy flip over, made her want to rub her legs together to ease the vague ache between them.

'Have you ever tried it?'

'No. But I'm guessing it could be, if you're the extrovert type.'

'And you're not.'

'We're not talking about me.' She hastily busied herself with her drink.

'We are now,' Niccolo said lazily. 'If I had a karaoke evening, would you take to the stage and try it out?' He laughed when she looked at him with horror. 'Don't worry. Won't be happening, so you can stop trying to think of songs you like.' And then he caught himself wondering *what* songs she liked, *what* her taste in music was, and he was so disconcerted by the way his brain had veered off on that tangent that he frowned.

'No night life,' he said crisply. 'Although, of course, if any of the guests want to live it up there are drivers who can take them into the town. There are a couple of very good local bars if you fancy live music. So that's preconception number one you have to strike off the list.'

Ellie was relieved that she was no longer having to find ways of wriggling out of conversations she didn't like, yet strangely *disappointed*. She reminded herself that Niccolo

Rossi wasn't actually interested in *her,* although he readily gave the impression that he was. He was interested in what she could do for him, and that was why she had to make sure not to be lulled into thinking otherwise— because now and again he looked at her with those devastating eyes of his, smiled in a way that made her go hot and cold and murmured things in his sexy voice that sent shivers racing up and down her spine.

If she couldn't manage to control her physical reactions because her body was just idiotically disobedient, then she would have to make sure she controlled her *mind.*

'Noted,' she said, equally crisply. 'What will be the format of my stay in the resort? Are there any areas you'd particularly like me to focus on?'

'Not the guests,' Niccolo told her wryly. 'Like I said, they're largely a private bunch, and I doubt they'd like thinking that there's someone in their midst observing them.'

'But your members of staff know that I'm here on official business?' She blushed because that sounded ridiculous. This wasn't the scene of a crime and she wasn't an undercover investigator.

'They know you're with me having a look around.'

Ellie's brow pleated, but then she had been too wrapped up absorbing her surroundings to have paid much attention to exactly what he had said when she had been introduced to them.

'They don't know about your *official business*.' He grinned as he quoted back her words to her. 'People are rarely forthcoming if they think that someone is asking questions in an official capacity. And you might very well want to ask questions. So your cue is to blend in.' He looked at her, taking his time, in no hurry to break the silence. Then he said, voice brisk, 'What clothes have you brought with you?'

'Sorry?'

'Clothes? What have you brought? Please don't tell me that your suitcase is stuffed with an assortment of navy and grey suits.'

'Of course not!' Two bright patches of colour stained her cheeks. She hadn't brought suits, but neither had she brought sarongs, and she guessed that sarongs would be the sort of wardrobe he might consider appropriate. Too bad. He might not want her broadcasting that she was here to work, but she was. And that had been foremost in her mind when she had done her packing.

'Because the only place you could possibly

blend in if you show up in a series of starchy suits would be an office.'

'I guess I could be your secretary.' She slid her eyes over his beautifully sculpted face, over his ferociously well-honed physique, and wondered what it might be like working for him. The thought of having to have her defences up twenty-four-seven sent a shiver down her spine and she was relieved when he shot that suggestion down in flames without bothering to consider it.

'Wouldn't work. The last time I was here, I came with my secretary. Engineering a long winded fabrication about why she might have been replaced would be impractical.' Niccolo gazed at her with hooded eyes. 'Perhaps you could be one of the guests,' he murmured, trying to imagine her eyeing up the men with a view to bedding them, and strangely not liking the thought of it.

'No. That's out of the question. I don't see why I have to pretend to be anyone at all. I promise you I'll be discreet. If I need to find out anything, then I'm more than capable of working it into the conversation in a casual manner. Besides, I'm not in the market for any kind of relationship, and I would feel uncomfortable pretending that I might be.'

'So you've come here with me,' Niccolo

mused, 'on my private jet, in the capacity of *no one in particular*. Even the most naïve person in the world would smell a rat, and I assure you my crew are anything but naïve.'

Ellie gazed at Niccolo helplessly and he gazed right back at her.

She had the most dewy, satiny skin he had ever seen. And the most expressive eyes. Right now those expressive eyes were staring at him with the intensity of something small and feeble caught in a trap.

Niccolo had honestly not thought ahead when it came to this whole set up. It was most unusual, and he knew that he should be doing his utmost to think things through in the most logical manner possible, but he was thoroughly enjoying himself.

It struck him forcibly just how preordained his entire life had been. From the very moment his father had died, he had known just what his future would be. He had never once questioned its restrictions, had indeed enjoyed the challenges posed, along with the satisfaction of knowing that he had risen to them.

But, yes, every step taken had been a step on a path carved out by the hand of fate. His one, single aberration on the personal front had made that path even more firmly cemented.

But now…

Veering from the path was intoxicating.

Who in their right mind wouldn't enjoy *intoxicating*?

'There *is* one obvious solution,' he thought aloud, voice pensive. 'You came with me.' He shrugged, dark eyes never straying for a second from her face. 'How hard would it be for you to stay with me?'

'Sorry? What? I don't understand.' Ellie was busy thinking that she had had no option *but* to come with him. She'd had no idea that it would involve a private jet, because in her world people just didn't do stuff like that, but what on earth did he mean by 'staying' with him? Where else was she going to stay? In a shed on the edge of the resort? In a tent on the nearest beach?

Niccolo must have read the confusion on her face and he explained slowly, coolly and in a tone of voice that implied that every word leaving his lips made irrefutable sense.

'You tell me that you don't want to assume the mantle of guest because you would feel uncomfortable with that masquerade but, like I said, my very private guests would not welcome any approach from someone they feel is intrusive. Many of them are notoriously publicity shy.'

'I get that,' Ellie agreed. 'And I certainly

would feel uncomfortable trying to quiz them about their experience under cover of curiosity. I can see that they might get suspicious and close up.'

'It could also damage the reputation I intend to cultivate for my resort as a place where privacy is respected. But, to get a feel for things, you would certainly need an introduction to the people who are paying to be here.'

'Yes...' Ellie sighed and chewed her lips thoughtfully. 'So... I could...er... Of course, I do know how to be tactful...'

'We're an item.' He shrugged. 'As my lover, any questions would be accepted as natural interest and answered without suspicion.'

'We're an *item*? I'm your *lover*?'

The undiluted horror in her voice instantly made his hackles rise. Granted this was a situation he had not predicted. Granted it shocked him as much as it evidently shocked her. And, yes, he did wonder what on earth had made him volunteer that as a solution, but now that the words were out of his mouth he was deeply affronted by her reaction.

Legions of women would have leapt with joy had that been presented to them as a solution to *anything*. Niccolo wasn't vain but neither was he unrealistic and he knew that what he brought to the table was considerable.

Except, the woman sitting opposite him was gaping open-mouthed at him as though he had just informed her that he was the carrier of something highly contagious and very, very nasty.

He scowled and fidgeted. Of their own accord, his eyes drifted from her full mouth, still parted in silent shock, down to the pale column of her neck, and then lower to the swell of her breasts underneath the extremely unfortunate and impractical outfit.

He wanted her. Was that why he had behaved out of character? Was that why he had suggested something that broke through all sensible barriers? Was he so used to having what he wanted when it came to women that he had subconsciously chosen an option that could be worked to his advantage?

Was she the embodiment of the irresistible challenge?

When was the last time he had had one of those?

When had he *ever* had one of those?

He felt a kick of excitement. His libido, which had been temporarily resting, awakened with vigour, reminding him that it had been a while since he had had sex. He slid down a little in the chair and adjusted his big body to ease the ferocious ache in his groin.

'Now that you're here,' he said gruffly, 'You're going to have to see for yourself what the atmosphere is like, what the people are like, what they enjoy doing. You're going to have to get the complete picture.'

Ellie's brain had frozen. He was saying something, of that she was aware, but she wasn't taking any of it in because she was still reeling in shock at what he had just said.

How had her life managed to move from pitching for a job to being asked to pretend to be involved with a billionaire?

She sneaked a glance at him, to see whether she had misinterpreted a situation. Their eyes tangled and she realised that he was being deadly serious.

'You're mad,' was her response to that.

'It makes sense.' Unaccustomed to losing at anything, Niccolo wasn't going to lose now. Being told that he was mad was not going to encourage him gracefully to back down.

'In what world does it make sense?' Ellie gasped. 'We don't even know one another!'

'If you're wandering here, having arrived with me on my private jet for no discernible reason, you're going to spook the guests and you're going to get tongues wagging amongst my members of staff. If you spook the guests, you could end up losing me their business.

They come here to avoid publicity, not to court it. They'll think I've brought a journalist here to spy on them, and you know what they say about word of mouth.'

Appalled, Ellie stared at him. Nothing he said made sense even though everything he said seemed very logical.

'This is crazy,' was all she could find to say.

Niccolo wondered how he had managed to find himself in a situation of having to persuade a reluctant woman into *pretending* to have a relationship with him. The pulsing ache in his loins and the drift of his imagination as he looked at her natural, unadorned prettiness answered the question.

'You should have thought about this before you dragged me out here!' Ellie hissed angrily, careful to keep her voice down, leaning towards him, then pulling back because, the closer she got, the more she felt the tug of something that screamed *danger*.

Her heart was thumping inside her like a sledgehammer. Her skin was burning hot, prickly and uncomfortable. She wished she could blame it on her poor choice of clothing but she couldn't.

Just the thought of getting close to that danger filled her with dread—and something else that was terrifying.

'I never signed up to this when I came here!' she cried.

'The mark of true creativity is an ability to think on one's feet.'

'I'm thinking that this is a ridiculous situation!'

'What are you so afraid of?'

'I'm not afraid of *anything*.'

'As my partner, you will be able to get all the information you need to build a really good campaign for me, one that incorporates the subtleties of the resort and what it offers. You'll have the chance to change some of your hard and fast preconceptions. You should be seeing this as an opportunity and a challenge instead of trying to run away like a coward.'

'I'm not *running away like a coward*!' Ellie gasped indignantly.

'Seize the day,' Niccolo urged, liking the way her eyes glittered when she was angry. 'There is little I appreciate more than someone who can adapt to unforeseen circumstances and use them to their advantage. Take this on and you will certainly have my guaranteed attention when it comes to future advertising campaigns for my companies. As you know, I have extensive business concerns.'

'No one would believe for a second that I'm anything other than your employee,' she pointed out, making herself think like him, without emotion, rationally, coolly.

'Opposites occasionally attract.' Niccolo shrugged, lounging back in his chair and watching the play of emotion on her face with brooding intensity.

Ellie bared her teeth in a polite smile. 'Perhaps it would be best if I returned to London.'

'Are you prepared to refuse this contract, and the vast potential advertising portfolio that could come with it, off your own bat?'

Ellie hesitated. Was she? She was a partner in the agency, with the power to judge situations and make decisions, but she had come this far—was she really and truly prepared to walk away now from the pot of gold? She glared at him, trapped by his logic, desperate to wriggle free and yet not knowing how.

'You're here for a week,' Niccolo told her softly. 'Why don't you live a little and take a risk? Do you imagine that you have anything to fear from me?'

'Of course I don't,' Ellie said uncomfortably.

Take a risk? Ever since she'd been confronted by him pumping iron in a gym her whole life had felt risky and she hated the feeling.

'If you imagine that I'm going to suddenly start making a nuisance of myself, then you're quite mistaken,' Niccolo murmured, watching carefully as denial and doubt turned to embarrassment.

'I never thought… I would never suggest that…that you would make a nuisance of yourself…' Ellie stammered, mortified at the wry amusement in his dark eyes.

'Naturally we would be expected to share accommodation,' he murmured, lowering his eyes but very clearly picturing her aghast expression at the unfolding of a nightmare scenario. 'Which works, incidentally, because there are far more guests here than I originally expected. Freeing up a villa for you would require some expert juggling.'

Who would have imagined that the thing that was not easily accessible could be so powerfully tempting? Okay, so maybe a deal… Yes, he could understand why and how he might pursue a deal in the face of fierce opposition. But a woman? What was that about?

And would he have been tempted if he had truly believed that there was nothing between them?

No.

There was something there, something hot and simmering in a place she was barely aware of. He sensed it and it was as powerful as a live electric charge. Her eyes on him were as assessing as his were on her, even if she had no intention of admitting it.

'I refuse to share anything with you,' Ellie said vehemently, her anger spiralling a few more notches, because he remained unruffled by her agitated protests.

'I repeat,' Niccolo drawled, 'Do you imagine I would ever make a nuisance of myself?'

'That's not the point.'

'You shared my private jet with me.'

'That's not the same and you know it.'

Niccolo shrugged. 'I have my own private villa here. Out of bounds for guests. It's a four-bedroomed plantation house. Think we might be jostling for space if we shared it?'

'Why would you have a four-bedroomed villa here?' Ellie demanded suspiciously and Niccolo burst out laughing.

'Because I can,' he told her mildly. 'So I do. Who knows when something like that can come in handy? Care to see whether it's big enough for the both of us? Because, if you choose to dig your heels in, then you're free to go back to London and explain that you blew a fortune in possible contracts out of the water.'

'That's blackmail.' Ellie paused. 'And why are you so determined that I fall in line with what you're suggesting? Isn't it just going to cause complications for you?'

Niccolo gave that some serious thought. Complications? The last woman he'd temporarily had in his life had involved complications and she hadn't been the first. Complications came from women who wanted more than he was prepared to give.

In comparison, this was flirting. Ellie was interested in him and he was interested in her. Scratch the surface, and that was about the size of it. But he wasn't her type. She'd made that perfectly clear. No, there would be no complications on that front.

He wasn't going to try and seduce her, but there was a strong possibility that the chemistry between them would ignite, and he wouldn't fight to put out the fire.

Maybe she would see that not all relationships were worthless because they weren't destined for the long term.

Niccolo knew that he could try and dig up a thousand reasons for doing what he was doing but, in the end, the biggest pull was that, for the first time in a very long time indeed, he was having fun.

CHAPTER FIVE

APPARENTLY NOT. APPARENTLY there would be no complications. Apparently it was a straight-forward solution to an unexpected situation.

Apparently, apparently, apparently.

Ellie's objections, even to her own ears, sounded feeble. Niccolo had a way of making what was a crazy situation sound perfectly acceptable. They would share his private villa. It was big enough to sleep eight. Where, he had asked patiently, was the problem? From the vantage point of being 'involved' with him, she would be able to get a real feel for the place. It was necessary because this was a template for other resorts. Get it right and his venture would take off. Get it wrong and it could be damaged permanently. A lot would rest on tapping into just the right approach. Not sleazy but not sun-set and roses. Something in between. And she could only get what that *something* was if she immersed herself in the atmosphere.

And, to do that, she would need to mingle with the staff and with the guests.

But from a non-threatening, privileged position. She had declined the suggestion that she simply absorb the atmosphere from the perspective of guest. She was not interested in the possibility of anyone making a play for her. Fair enough. She could not see a way of tactfully quizzing the guests about their motivations for being there. Also fair enough. How many more 'fair enough's were there? His suggestion should not have the fear factor that it did but she still quailed at the prospect of sharing space with him under the pretence of being involved with him.

Her panicked concerns had been dealt with in a way that had made her feel a little foolish for raising them in the first place.

Which was why, drinks finished, they sauntered under the stars towards his villa which was in a secluded section of the resort.

Night had fallen on the island, and a tropical star-lit sky would have been romantic in any other scenario but, with a stomach knotted with tension, Ellie stood on the threshold of the villa with her heart in her mouth.

'Don't look as though you're about to face the hangman's noose,' Niccolo told her.

'I honestly don't think anyone is going to buy

this crazy story.' Ellie gave one final, feeble pro-
test before stepping into the magnificent villa.

On this count, at least, he had been one hundred percent truthful. The villa was absolutely
enormous.

Hot, sticky, confused and out of her depth,
Ellie could still appreciate the magnificence of
a place for which no expense had been spared.

It sat in its own grounds, which at this time
of the night was alive with the call of frogs,
crickets and a busy, background orchestra of
insect noises that was strangely peaceful. In
the distance, the sea joined the chorus, a faraway ebb and flow of the ocean. The villa itself
was surrounded by a huge wooden veranda.
Painted cream, there was nothing to mar the
view that in the morning would be revealed
from all sides, which respectively gave out over
the ocean, the manicured lawns and a back-
drop of lush mountain. Bamboo trees reached
up towards the velvety black sky, swaying like
stilts in the breeze, creaking and rustling as
though talking to one another in a language
only they could understand.

She glimpsed a floodlit infinity swimming
pool.

It was a thousand times bigger than her own
apartment, yet the tight knot of tension in the
pit of her stomach only increased as she en-

tered the villa, where her bag was sitting neatly alongside his own far more expensive, beaten leather case with its distinctive designer logo in one corner.

'My bag is here! Why is my bag here? Did you know that I would end up with no choice but to agree to this...this...crazy situation?'

'Default position,' Niccolo said, without a hint of apology. 'You hadn't been allocated a villa.' He began walking quickly round the villa, his sharp eyes missing nothing. He noted the quality of the furnishings, the standard of the kitchen, the size of the air-conditioning units.

He took in *everything*, while Ellie traipsed behind him, as uncomfortable as it was possible to be in clothes that were ludicrously inappropriate.

'What do you think?' He spun round and, startled, she took a few steps back, eyes wide.

'You know what I think,' she began in a shaky voice. 'That this is not at all appropriate! I had no idea that I would be asked to partake in a ridiculous charade when I agreed to come over here!'

'About the villa,' Niccolo expanded, without batting an eye. 'What do you think about the quality of the workmanship?'

Ellie reddened and glared at him.

'In the face of a *fait accompli*, if that's what

you want to call it—although I assure you this is something I had not bargained for—I suggest you stop moaning and move on. Now, why don't you put on your work hat, to match the work outfit, and give me your professional opinion on the villa? The rest are nowhere near as big as this but the fittings are all exactly the same.'

Ellie was mortified that she was being given a dressing down, being reminded that she was here in a work capacity, being told to handle herself like a professional adult.

Anyone else, given the circumstances, would have had their eye on the main chance and thought nothing of what Niccolo had suggested. Instead, she had gone into an instant meltdown, had put him in a position where he had had to assure her that she was safe from him and had shrieked and protested like a distraught virgin on a ship full of marauding pirates.

He had given her and the agency the benefit of the doubt. He had seen past the soft-focus allure she had brought to a campaign which, for him, had not been realistic enough in promoting the virtues of his resort, and offered her the opportunity of acquiring first-hand knowledge of what his hotel chain would be all about so that she could alter her pitch accordingly.

She was surprised that he hadn't considered

the problem of *how* she was going to acquire that knowledge without appearing inquisitive. Maybe he'd thought that she would choose to blend in as one of the guests, but her horror at that prospect had propelled him into another solution.

At any rate, as he said, she was here now and there was no point yelling for the smelling salts and wailing that it was a crazy solution.

And to put him in the position of declaring his lack of interest in her! As if a man who could have any woman he wanted would pay her a blind bit of notice!

Ellie burned with shame. She was overreacting, and of course she knew why. It was because he made her feel uncomfortable in her own skin, restless and *aware*. He made her whole body tingle and, when he was around, she was horribly, uncomfortably conscious of a fierce sexuality she hadn't known existed.

She felt *scared* when she thought about sharing space with him. And when she thought about sharing space with him in the capacity of fake girlfriend she practically wanted to swoon like a Victorian maiden.

The way to deal with this was to tune him out as a man—a *sinfully sexy* man—and relegate him to position of business colleague. A bit like her partners in the firm, both of whom were very happily married, and both of whom she had never looked at once in any way other than as talented, ambitious guys who brainstormed with her and treated her like a talented equal, despite her relative youth.

'The fittings are all magnificent.' She walked away from him and really devoted her attention to the spectacular villa, which was a marvel of wood, cream voile, at the huge windows that were flung open to allow in every breath of sea breeze, muted, soft colours and sofas hand-made from the local wood and bamboo with big, spongy cushions. Interested, she inspected the kitchen, the veranda and all the other rooms on the ground floor, asking questions about the other villas and vaguely thinking that it was actually the sort of resort where, contrary to what she had thought, a guest could come and relax and ignore everyone else there, but as a single person would not be surrounded by couples or families.

She could see that it could be relaxing rather than pressurised.

'And what's the agenda for while I'm here?' She turned to him at the foot of the wooden staircase, with its pale grey runner that led up to a series of bedrooms and bathrooms.

Niccolo lounged against the wall, towering over her, hands shoved into his pockets.

'First off the bat, I show you to your room.'

Ellie said nothing but every nerve inside her body screamed with tension as she followed him up the stairs and into a bedroom that was decorated in the same style as the rooms they had left behind. Wooden floors, billowing voile at the windows, an overhead fan and a fantastically beautiful king-sized bed with a soft mosquito net draped over it.

He had carried her case up and he dumped it on the bed now and looked around him for a few seconds before his dark eyes rested on her face.

'You're hot and tired,' he said, and Ellie shot him a wry smile, because that had to be the understatement of the century.

'Is it that obvious?'

'And you're alarmed at being put in a position you hadn't banked on. I get that. I'm not a fan of the unexpected either.'

Ellie softened, because his voice was low and sincere. 'I like to know what I'm getting into. I like to be prepared for all situations.'

'And that, unfortunately, isn't always possible.'

'How am I supposed to behave if we're *an item*?' Ellie asked with genuine interest and more than a little apprehension.

For a few seconds, Niccolo was confounded.

She wasn't attacking him, and the way she was staring at him, with a slightly perplexed frown, made her look an awful lot younger than a woman in her mid- to late twenties. She looked like a teenager—sweet sixteen and never been kissed.

But of course she'd been kissed.

Had boyfriends. Made love. Even if none of those lovers had managed to scatter the stardust she seemed to be looking for.

Hadn't she? Surely! The way she had earnestly regaled him with her high moral code and her mystifying 'love for ever' mantra nudged the crazy notion into his head that she might be far more untouched than most women her age. Certainly the ones *he* had been involved with over the years.

A warning bell sounded somewhere. It could have been elevator music for all the attention Niccolo paid to it.

'I'm not going to run around gazing at you in a besotted fashion and holding hands,' she said tartly, and Niccolo grinned.

'Is that how you behave when you're an item with someone?' He raised his eyebrows and laughed. 'Don't worry. I'm not into star gazing and holding hands.'

'Aren't you?'

'I prefer to leave that to the eternal romantics. I take a more pragmatic approach to relationships.'

Ellie knew that what he thought about relationships was none of her business and yet, in an odd way, wasn't she here to promote a project that *dealt* with relationships? 'Is that why you believe that casual hook-ups are all right? Because of your pragmatic approach?'

'Let's put it this way,' Niccolo drawled. 'The only certainty in life is financial security. Look after your finances and they'll never let you down. The same can't be said for relationships. My guests will come here in search of something—a companion, a lover, a permanent fixture in their life, a dream, a hope. Who knows? I provide the sort of environment where all those things are a possibility. If some find that a casual relationship presents itself, then good for them. Even if it doesn't end up going anywhere.

'You really can't hide your disapproval, can you? You'll just have to judge for yourself. You might find that the resort is full of very happy and contented men and women who are looking for sex without strings attached, or sex with only a few strings attached.'

Ellie snorted. 'I don't understand what "sex with only a few strings attached" is. I know all about sex with no strings. That's the typical relationship where a man makes sure the words "permanent", "tomorrow" or "in the future" never accidentally cross his lips.'

Niccolo grinned and lounged indolently against the door. She'd certainly summed it up nicely. He couldn't think when those words had last crossed his lips.

'So,' Ellie demanded, 'I'm curious as to what the *few strings* are.'

'Okay…give me a minute or two and I'll get back to you on that one.' He was still grinning and the lazy amusement in his eyes sent a buzz of awareness rippling through her.

Night-black collided with cool hazel and for a second their eyes tangled, leaving her breathless.

She frantically found the thread of her disapproval and seized upon it with heartfelt relief. 'Maybe the so-called *strings* involve some poor woman cooking your meals before you dispatch her back to the dating pool.'

'No, definitely no strings of the sort you're describing.' Niccolo laughed with an elegant, rueful gesture. 'I've never encouraged any woman to familiarise herself with the layout of my kitchen.'

'Because you enjoy cooking yourself?' Ellie tried and failed to picture the arrogant, impossibly sexy man in front of her being a New Age guy who shared the household chores and enjoyed getting behind a stove. In fact, she tried and failed to imagine any apartment he lived in actually having a kitchen at all.

'Proud to say, I've never explored that avenue.' Niccolo was tickled pink at the ebb and flow of colour in her cheeks. She was so easy to rile and it took more willpower than he possessed not to continually rise to the occasion. 'Maybe you're right,' he mused truthfully, surprised to find himself, just for a second, forsaking the ease of banter to give her a heartfelt response. 'Maybe there's no such thing as a relationship with just *some* strings attached. Maybe there are either no strings or a complete ball of string unravelling into eternity.'

'And you're a no-strings kind of guy.' Ellie thought that, for all his devastating good looks and charismatic charm, he really was the last sort of man in the world she could ever fall for. Yes, there was some kind of weird physical appeal that defied all common sense, but beyond that was just the sort of man she scorned, the sort of man for whom commitment was a dirty word. He was right about financial security being important but emotional security was equally as important.

'I feel sorry for the women who decide to go out with you,' she ventured thoughtfully, staring off into the distance, pulled back to her ever-changing past where stability had spelt boring and physical attraction was something to be indulged, whatever the consequences.

'Why?'

'Because I can imagine you leave jars of broken hearts behind you.'

'And that's where you're going to have to try and revisit your mind-set.'

'What are you talking about?'

'When you stroll around, chatting to my guests, it might be an idea not to give in to the temptation to preach to them about the misery of life without a wedding ring on their finger. Try and avoid playing the judgement card.'

'I told you I would keep an open mind and I meant it.' But Ellie flushed, conscious of the fact that what she saw as morally upright he saw as dangerously narrow-minded.

She wanted this job—the agency would take wings and fly into the outer stratosphere if she landed it—and as a consequence Niccolo did as he had hinted at and poured other work their way.

To get the job she had to fight down her natural inclination to be dismissive about the whole concept of his resort and look at it through different eyes. Or, at the very least, she had to stop shooting her mouth off and persuade him that, yes, she knew where he was coming from with the concept.

'Glad to hear it.' Niccolo straightened. Looked at her coolly and neutrally. 'Now I expect, after all the shocks to your system, the last thing you want is to explore the resort with me in the role of my girlfriend. Fortunately, exhaustion is a very good excuse for retiring for the evening.'

For a brief moment, Ellie had actually forgotten the whole 'phoney girlfriend' situation but now it came back to her in a rush and the knot in her stomach reappeared at speed.

The villa was enormous. There was no question that the charade would leave her in the awkward position of having to jostle for space alongside him when they were inside. They could practically set up camps on opposite sides and never cross paths unless accidentally.

Which wasn't going to happen, but at least once inside the villa they could be the business colleagues that they were and could agree when and where to meet so that they could discuss and debrief.

And it was only going to be for a matter of days.

'I *am* exhausted. Tomorrow? Perhaps you could let me know order of events.'

'Hard to plan in advance.'

'I will need some time during the day to work on the campaign.'

'Don't worry. You'll have ample time to bury yourself in your work,' Niccolo told her wryly, once again piqued by her obvious lack of enthusiasm to be in his company unless absolutely necessary. 'You're not going to be chained to my side. Anyone who knows anything about me would know that that's not how I operate, so you'll find you have lots of free time to do your own thing. At any rate, I'll be busy checking out behind the scenes, making sure the electrics aren't going to fail or the walls aren't going to fall down. My people will have taken care of everything but I'm the boss. I'll have to spend time prodding and poking.'

'Oh, that's a relief.' Then she half-smiled sheepishly. 'Sorry. I didn't mean that to sound the way it did.'

There was nothing Niccolo found amusing about a confession that couldn't have been further from the truth but he managed something like a smile in return. 'The days kick off early in the tropics,' he said abruptly. 'I very much doubt you'll be tempted to lie in.'

'I'm a morning person.' Ellie decided that this was a perfect opportunity to lay down some rules and regulations, because she could very easily find herself bobbing and drifting in unfamiliar waters, which was something that just seemed to happen in Niccolo's presence. One minute she could be comfortably discussing work-related matters and then, without warning, she would be floundering in a whirlpool of treacherous prying, personal questions that made her anxious and uncertain. The man didn't play by the rules, and he was unpredictable, and a week of that wasn't going to do. At least, not if she was going to emerge with her blood pressure and nervous system intact.

'I wonder why I'm not shocked to hear that?' Niccolo murmured under his breath.

'And I'm not here to lie in and enjoy late mornings. I'm here to work and you needn't be worried that I'm going to forget that for a moment.'

'I wasn't.'

'Perhaps we could loosely agree on a timetable whereby we discuss the day ahead over breakfast, and then I'll wander around and not just get a feel for the place, but ascertain the most scenic shots that could be used in an extensive visual campaign, perhaps targeting the upmarket tourist trade. People are heavily influenced by photographs, so I'll make it a priority to go beyond the obvious scenic shots and really try and encompass things that tell a slightly different story of what it would be like to come out here for a short break.'

Niccolo thought that, animated as she was now, she was even more attractive. His eyes lingered on the shadow of a dimple on one side of her mouth, which appeared when she smiled, and the way her hazel eyes lit up, as clear as polished glass.

'We could loosely agree to have breakfast around eight-thirty,' he murmured. 'There's the option of having it delivered to us here, which would probably be the preferred choice, were we star-struck lovers…'

'But as we're not…' Ellie's skin burned at the image that shot into her head at those carelessly delivered words, an image of Niccolo as a *lover*, hot and hard and burning with passion. She gulped. 'As we're not…' She cleared her throat and shuffled because the heat that swept through her was proof of just how powerful those images in her head were. 'We could meet at the…hotel restaurant…'

'But for tonight…' Niccolo glanced at his watch '…feel free to order in anything you want. The fridge is also stocked with basics. I'm going to touch base with some of my people here and find out what's left to be done and how the guest list is shaping up. Is there anything you need before I leave?'

'No.' She was looking forward to him clearing off. She really was. She couldn't wait to be on her own because, when she was around him, she was manoeuvring through a minefield. She very definitely *did not* feel a certain sense of emptiness at the prospect of several much needed hours on her own. Without having to spar with him. Without wondering what conversational ambush he was going to lead her into. Without bristling because he was either laughing at her or deliberately making her feel uncomfortable.

'In that case, I'm off and I'll see you tomorrow morning. We can reconvene by the front door.'

Ellie got the impression he was laughing at her, although his lean face was serious. 'That sounds brilliant,' she told him vaguely.

'And,' Niccolo added, lowering his voice, which did dangerous things to her equilibrium, 'just for the record—and I'm only saying this because, as my girlfriend, it's something you should know...'

'I'm not your girlfriend!'

Niccolo ignored the interruption. 'You really shouldn't feel sorry for any of the women I've dated in the past. I'm excellent when it comes to knowing what it takes to make sure my woman is happy.'

Ellie went beetroot-red. 'I'm sure you'll find that…that…women want love and commitment,' she stuttered, furiously embarrassed.

'And for those, they have only themselves to blame, because I always state from the outset that those are two things that are not on the table. However…'

Ellie stared into the smouldering depths of his deep, dark eyes and was overcome by a sensation of drowning. Her brain was telling her to snap out of it and confront him with the derision that remark deserved—to inform him coldly and firmly that washing his hands of commitment before embarking on a sexual adventure with a woman did not make him a hero. Her body, however, was responding in a way that was wildly out of control. She blinked and opened and shut her mouth, goldfish-style. Niccolo gazed at her until her whole treacherous body was burning up.

'However?' was all she could croak.

'*However,* I'm generous to a fault, and not just when it comes to cars and jewellery.'

'There's more to generosity,' Ellie managed to point out, dry though her mouth was, 'Than cars and jewellery.'

'Indeed there is, and that's what I'm talking about. Well done to you for honing in on that.' He smiled slowly and his dark eyes glittered with just the sort of wicked, wicked intent that made her want to whimper. 'I'm generous where it matters. In bed. Between the sheets.' He lowered his eyes and then, when he next spoke, his voice was crisp and business-like, while Ellie had to mentally shake herself down, agonisingly conscious that she had been hanging onto his every word like a teenager in the grip of an adolescent crush.

'See you in the morning!' Niccolo wanted her so badly right now that his body *hurt*. Did she have any idea at all how dangerously appealing those expressive eyes were? How little it would take for a man like him, highly sexed and highly experienced, to cover her parted lips with his and show her just how hot his generosity could be?

Ellie frowned, hurt because she knew that she was being dismissed. He looked positively anxious to be on his way.

And that, she told herself as he swung round on his heels, slamming shut the door behind him, should be a vital lesson in making sure she didn't lose focus while she was out here.

She had no idea what to expect with them both living under one roof. She had visions of hearing him rattling around when he returned, reminding her that she wasn't alone in the villa, but as it turned out she was able to prepare herself some fresh bread and cheese for dinner before taking to her bedroom, which not only had an *en suite* bathroom but an adjoining room that had been kitted out as a sitting room, complete with television and the facilities to work, including Internet access.

She planned to wake at the crack of dawn so that she could flick through the work she had brought with her and find a direction in which to move forward. It would give them both something to talk about over what would probably be a very stilted breakfast. She hoped that she wouldn't be expected to stare adoringly at him while she fiddled with a plate of scrambled eggs, and was reassured by what he had said about not being the kind of guy who walked around holding hands and whispering sweet nothings.

Niccolo struck her as just the sort of man who would see romantic gestures as pointless and risible. Romance, for him, would be getting his secretary to pick out an expensive item of jewellery, which the store would thoughtfully gift wrap so that his only contribution would be handing it over to the woman in question.

Then she remembered what he had said about his generosity and burned. Forget about the jewellery. That would probably only be a secondary concern to any woman he went out with. Who needed jewellery when they had the option of leading him by his designer tie straight into the nearest bed?

Mortified at the direction of her thoughts, Ellie looked at her phone to find that all her good intentions had been blown out of the water—she had overslept.

The woman who hadn't actually woken up later than seven in the morning since she'd been a teenager opened her eyes to find that it was after nine, at which point she sprang into action, throwing on the first thing that came to hand and bolting downstairs, too hot and bothered to wonder whether she would bump into Niccolo…and then not surprised to find an empty house because her adoring boyfriend clearly hadn't had the manners to hang around and wait for her to get out of bed.

She went outside and followed her nose in a sprawling resort that was largely still asleep.

The sun had already gathered pace and the skies were turquoise and cloud-free. In the distance, the sea glittered silvery-blue through banks of palm trees. The guests might still have been asleep, but the employees were up and about. Ellie nodded vaguely at some of them as she weaved her way around scattered cabanas and villas, none of which were anywhere as grand as the one she had just vacated, but all of which oozed luxury.

Here and there, some of the early risers were up and about. She glimpsed a swimming pool through the foliage, accessed down a winding flower-lined path. A couple of guests were reading, soaking up the sun. She wondered what the day would hold in store for them. Love? A soul mate? Exciting conversations with someone who might later become a fixture in their lives?

The more employees she spotted, the closer she knew she was to the main hotel building, which was hard to discern through the thickly landscaped gardens and the rows upon rows of palm trees.

Sure enough, she emerged into an open space, having walked for at least ten minutes. Almost immediately she spotted Niccolo, who was chatting at an outside table with two of his employees, who glanced at her as she approached.

He looked…beautiful. White linen shirt, rolled to the elbows, khaki shorts, loafers. Cool elegance. In the space of a few hours and with a change of scenery, he somehow looked more exotically foreign, his skin burnished bronze.

His slightly too-long hair gave him the look of a pirate and she had to make a conscious effort to propel herself forward, remembering to plaster a smile on her face the closer she got to him.

He was smiling back, perfectly at ease, although surely he was as uncomfortable with this awkward situation as she was?

She had no idea what was called for, but she didn't have time to work it out. He rose to his feet, tall and impossibly, compellingly attractive, and slung his arm round her shoulders, at which point Ellie forgot how to breathe.

Ellie wouldn't have been able to recall a single thing the two smiling English girls said to her. She knew she answered, and her face ached, which meant the smile was still in place.

But every nerve, muscle and tendon in her body was strained in electric awareness of the feel of his skin on hers.

Casual…proprietorial…and sending her body into crazy freefall.

Her nipples pinched, and between her legs burning heat was evidence of her body reacting with bewildering speed to his proximity.

And all she could think was, *Please don't let him know what's happening to me*.

CHAPTER SIX

SHE SURFACED TO find that the smiling English girls had gone and his hands had dropped back to his sides.

'I wondered whether you'd find me,' he told her, sitting down and gesturing to the chair opposite him, while one of the friendly staff bustled towards them to find out what they wanted. 'Not a creature was stirring,' he quipped, settling back and linking his fingers on his lap, 'when I got up at seven. Not even, as they say, a mouse. Far less a human.'

'You should have woken me,' Ellie mumbled, still in a daze from that casual physical touch. 'I never usually sleep late.'

'Nine's hardly late and you were probably jet-lagged.'

'Still… I apologise. I'm not here to laze around.'

'Let's not start the day with apologies.' He raised his eyebrows and grinned. 'Love means never having to say you're sorry. Remember?'

'Very funny.'

But he was still grinning after they'd given their orders for coffee and a breakfast of fresh bread and fried fish, a local speciality.

'I've had a few thoughts about the campaign,' Ellie began, determined to get cracking on the business front. 'The feel of the place is very different from what the photographs suggest. It's far more peaceful and a lot bigger than I thought it was going to be. I mean, a person could really get lost here.'

'That's the idea,' Niccolo drawled. 'Attention to privacy. Gives people the safety of knowing that they can choose to use my resort as a place to meet someone or simply come for the joy of relaxing without being surrounded by families. My employees liked you, by the way.'

Ellie blushed and fiddled with her cutlery as their breakfasts were placed in front of them, along with a jug of fresh coffee and a selection of fruit. 'Do all the staff know that I'm here in a professional capacity?'

'I did think about telling them, but I thought it fairer to spare them the bother of having to try and fudge answers if anyone showed any curiosity about you, so as far as they and mostly everyone else here is concerned, we're together.'

'Isn't that going to pose a problem…er… later?'

'No idea what you mean.'

'I'm only here for a week. What happens when we leave if they ask about me?'

Niccolo shrugged. 'Why would they ask?'

'Because they might be curious?'

'Eleanor…'

'Please call me Ellie.'

'Ellie…' He smiled gently. 'They're my employees, not the family priest in search of a confession. I've told them because I really didn't have much of a choice, but my private life isn't something they would question.'

Ellie nodded. Did she understand? Not really. She just assumed that he was so far up the pecking order that he could do whatever he wanted safe in the knowledge that, if anyone had an opinion about him, they would never dare share it, such was the extent of his power and his reach. He might be charm itself but only an idiot would take that at face value.

She changed the subject. 'If you've got stuff to do today—and I expect you have, from what you've told me—then I thought I might wander the grounds and touch base with some of the guests if they feel inclined to chat. Find out what drew them here in the first place.'

'Firstly, you're going to have to try a bit

harder to blend in with the wealthy set here.' Niccolo slung his napkin onto his empty plate and relaxed back. 'Please tell me that there are more colours to the wardrobe you've brought than navy-blue and white.' Her chestnut hair was tied back, just as it always was. She looked neat as a pin and about as relaxed as a busy worker-bee forced to have a day off honey-production duty, which pretty much summed it up.

Niccolo had never given much thought to how his lovers dressed. Now he realised that they had all been clones of one another. They'd worn small clothes to accentuate lingerie-model bodies. High heels to promote already long legs.

'I didn't come here for a holiday,' Ellie said defensively, well aware that blending in was impossible when she was wearing a navy-blue knee-length cotton skirt and a white sleeveless blouse, her only concession to the tropical surroundings being the sandals she had fished out of her cupboard and dusted down for the trip.

'But now here you are and whilst, admittedly, you're right insofar that you're not here on holiday, the circumstances are a little different than originally planned, wouldn't you agree?'

'I haven't got sundresses and sarongs,' Ellie imparted stiffly.

'But surely you must have had less formal attire for a trip to a hot country?'

'I haven't been on holiday abroad for years.' Ellie thought back to her wandering childhood and almost shuddered.

'That's unusual. Most people enjoy going on holiday.'

'Do you?'

'*Touché*. Although,' he said lazily, 'I do actually get around to relaxing every so often. Do you? Or is work your relaxation?' The deeper he dug, the more complex she became, and the more complex she became, the more he wanted to keep digging. 'What do you do for fun, Ellie?'

Ellie went bright-red. Why did she feel so defensive? It was a simple enough question. She could hardly expect him to stick to the brief twenty-four-seven, especially given the fact that he was not the sort of man who ever stuck to any brief of any kind if he didn't want to. More than anything else, the genuine curiosity in his voice made her question all sorts of things she didn't want to question. She realised that he had started making her question all sorts of things just by being the way he *was*. His emotional life might be the sort of emotional life she disliked but at least he had one.

'I've been focused on my career,' she heard herself say feebly.

'You're going to have to take the wardrobe up a notch,' Niccolo said bluntly. 'You look as though you should be quizzing the guests about their tax returns rather than relaxing and having fun in the sun.'

Unexpectedly, that hurt a lot more than Ellie thought possible. She imagined the sort of women Niccolo dated and they didn't look like tax inspectors.

'There are a couple of boutiques on the island,' he said. 'Purely catering to the wealthy tourists. And there are a couple in the hotel complex, as a matter of fact.'

'I can't afford to spend money on clothes that'll only last a few days!' Ellie was appalled at that sort of extravagance.

'Consider it on the house. It's the very least I could do for the woman I'm dating. Finished?' He nodded to her empty plate. 'What did you think of the breakfast? Food will be as important as the scenery at a place like this. Only the finest will do.'

'Delicious.' Some of the guests were filtering into the dining area. They were largely on their own, carrying beach bags and books. And, to her surprise, none of them seemed to be under the age of forty.

'Not quite the raging orgy you imagined, is it?' Niccolo murmured drily, leaning into her.

None of the guests looked their way with any curiosity. They all had the studied indifference to the people around them of the very wealthy. Two guests strolled in, both in their early sixties, sat together and seemed to compare books.

'Now, I did have some plans for today, but I think a trip to the town is going to be on the cards.'

Ellie blinked and focused on the man in front of her. She'd always prided herself on her open-mindedness. Of course, she had objected to the principle of Niccolo's resort. She had had no idea just how far from reality her assumptions were. These people would not be sneaking behind the bushes to sate their libidos. This was match-making at its most discreet.

As the guests continued to arrive, some of them drifting to other parts of the hotel, Ellie was forced to re-evaluate the sweeping assumptions she had made. She could see why Niccolo had liked the gentility of her campaign, but why he had felt it necessary to bring her to the resort so that she could see for herself where improvements could be made.

She felt the thrill of excitement at the job facing her. Niccolo's dark eyes were warm with appreciation and she knew, in an instant, that he could read exactly what was going through her head.

It scared her.

'Please don't,' she whispered, and for a few seconds, as their eyes tangled, she lost track of what she meant by that.

'Please don't do what?' Niccolo returned, his voice low and husky, sending a shiver of unbearable awareness through her, as powerful as the sizzle of a branding iron on virgin flesh. 'Look at you?'

This isn't real, her mind screamed. *This isn't flirting—this is playing a part for the sake of appearances. This is about building a fiction in front of his guests just in case...*

But the lazy intensity of his dark eyes was wreaking havoc with her common sense and sending her body into frantic, fevered overdrive.

Her nipples pinched into tight, sensitive buds and her breasts were heavy and painful. She wanted him to touch them, caress them, take them in his hands and massage them. She wanted his mouth all over her, licking, teasing and rousing.

Ellie felt faint. If she stood up, she knew she would end up falling, because her legs wouldn't be able to support her.

Her mouth was dry. She was peering over the edge of a precipice, swaying in the wind, dizzy and sick as she looked down, down, down.

'Please don't change your plans for me,' she managed to croak.

Niccolo didn't say anything. The atmosphere between them was static. Did she feel it? Of course she did! Her fingers were playing convulsively with her napkin and her body language was saying it all.

She was as jumpy as a cat on a hot tin roof and her eyes were flicking between him and those nervous, nervous fingers.

It gave him a buzz that sent his blood pressure into the stratosphere and reminded him of what hot pursuit could feel like. He'd forgotten. Ever since he'd set eyes on her, seen her skittishness, *smelled* the fragrant scent of uninvited and definitely unwanted desire, he'd felt stagnant senses come back to life.

He shifted. He was determined not to make a pass at her, but he wondered what he would do if she continued to ignore the pulsating chemistry between them. It was highly likely that she would, given her blinkered, prudish take on relationships.

Freezing showers into the foreseeable future held no appeal.

He stood up, not giving her the option of

backing away. 'If we head off now, we can hit
those shops as soon as they open, and then the
remainder of the day is free.'

'But I can't...'

'You need to start thinking *I can* instead of
I can't,' Niccolo pronounced firmly, and Ellie
glared at him, because she had never been ac-
cused of shying away from challenges in her
life before. Unfortunately, in his presence, the
'can't's definitely outweighed the 'can's. 'You
don't have to dig into your savings for a handful of clothes that you'll wear for a week and
then send to a charity shop. I will cover the
cost and you can call that client privilege, especially as you're in the position of needing
a new wardrobe due to circumstances not of
your own making.'

'I don't need a new wardrobe.' Protesting
was akin to being strapped on a railway track
and hoping that the oncoming train was somehow going to pirouette over your tightly bound
body.

She watched helplessly for a few seconds
and then tripped after him, almost bumping
into him when he stopped and turned to her.
He took her by the shoulders and examined her
critically from the crown of her head to the tips
of her toes, then back up again.

'You're the only woman I've ever met who

has begged *not* to be given the chance to buy a new wardrobe when someone else has offered to pay for it.'

'That's the point, though,' Ellie muttered awkwardly. 'I'd be more comfortable if I were paying for it myself. Besides, it's insulting to be told that you're not good enough.'

'When did I ever say that?' Niccolo asked, utterly serious. Gone was the husky, sexy banter. His voice was cool, his eyes shuttered and unreadable. He began walking, allowing her to keep pace with him as they left the hotel and headed towards a bank of all-white two-seater off-road cars that were parked like a row of soldiers against a brick wall that was coloured red and orange with clambering, tropical flowers.

He opened the passenger door for her and slid round into the driver's seat, but as soon as he'd fired up the engine he turned to her, and when he spoke his voice was still cool.

'Don't take your personal hang-ups out on me.' He held her gaze until she wanted to squirm in embarrassment, like a schoolchild being ticked off by the principal. 'If you have insecurities, then that's your business. The suggestion that you might welcome some clothes was a practical one. If it offends your feminist sensibilities, then we'll head straight back into the hotel and you can hide behind your tablet and your files and pretend that you feel comfortable walking around in your utterly impractical navy-blue skirt and buttoned-up-to-the-throat blouse.'

Ellie broke the connection and turned away, chewing nervously on her lip.

Her clothes *were* impractical, and not just because they didn't suit her improbable role as girlfriend to a billionaire. They were impractical because they were uncomfortable in the searing heat. She had not banked on the humidity or the intensity of the sun because, in her head, she had somehow thought that she would be dealing with the sort of polite, barely there heat of an English summer.

Her outfits were all along the lines of what she was now wearing, and what she was now wearing felt itchy and uncomfortable.

But a change of wardrobe was something she had found frankly terrifying and she knew why. Whether she was pretending to be Niccolo's girlfriend or not, boundaries could remain in place if she could continue to hide behind her sensible workman-like outfits, outfits that screamed, *I'm here to do a job, whatever the changed circumstances.* When she was gripping her tablet, with all its reports, work files and accounting projections, she was safe.

But when she thought of colourful clothes,

and sarongs and flowers in her hair, the last pieces of armour that were protecting her would be removed and then where would that leave her?

She looked at the grim lines of Niccolo's lean, ridiculously beautiful face, the hint of stubble darkening his bronzed skin, and she shivered.

'I just feel as though I came here to do a job and now I'm on a rollercoaster ride and I can't get off.'

'Some people welcome rollercoaster rides.' Niccolo tilted her face so that she was looking at him, and Ellie blushed.

'I'm not one of those people,' she blurted out. 'My life was one big rollercoaster ride when I was growing up, and ever since then I've avoided them like the plague.' She gasped because she hadn't meant to say that. 'But my clothes *are* impractical,' she hurried on, mortified at giving away a slice of her private life when she was usually so reticent at sharing her past with anyone. 'And I apologise if I somehow came across as being ungrateful for the offer. I'm not. It's very…well…very generous of you…' She tapered off into uncomfortable silence, dreading him picking up the threads of a conversation she didn't want to pursue, because she didn't want to talk about herself.

He didn't.

'Glad we're on the same page,' he purred, reversing out of the slot and swinging the car away from the hotel. He began talking about an ambitious project to incorporate a guide book on the island linked to his resort. Ellie's nerves settled. She kicked back and appreciated the scenery as the car bumped its way round bends, with each new corner heralding a fresh burst of colour. She listened to him, and itched to get her fingers on a key board, because there was so much she would be able to write about the stunning island they were navigating.

'You're really in this for more than just profit, aren't you?' She turned to him, her hazel eyes alight with enthusiasm, and Niccolo glanced across at her.

The windows were down and the breeze had ruffled her hair loose from its clips, pins and elastic. Strands whipped across her face and her cheeks were pink from the heat.

'I volunteered to be on the tourist board when I was given permission to build my resort,' he murmured absently, tearing his eyes away from her face so that he could concentrate on the business of driving. 'My hotel might provide jobs, but it was never my intention to set up shop in this glorious part of the world so that I could take advantage of the natural beauty and make money out of it without ensuring that the island benefited. And I'm not just talking about improved employment prospects for a few locals.'

Everything he said contradicted the image Ellie had formed in her head of a ruthless, maverick playboy who was in it purely for the money.

'You want to expand the tourist industry,' she said slowly, realising the scale of his ambition.

'It would help the island.' He shrugged and looked sideways at her. 'We'll be in the town in a handful of minutes. You'll see that there is a dire need for improvements in the infrastructure. There's also the potential for more development in the farming industry. All that can be achieved if tourism is cultivated.'

Hanging onto his every word, Ellie was really only aware of her surroundings when the vehicle drew to a stop and, blinking, she saw that they were parked on a hill, below which, on either side, the main street sprawled with a combination of modern offices, straggling shops and lots of vendors on the pavements selling a dizzying array of fresh fruit and vegetables.

It was packed. On a wall, a group of teenagers was laughing and joking. There were people hanging out, chatting. Off the main street, she could see a side road, and beyond that an open square in which a market was in full swing.

A solid wall of heat hit her as soon as she stepped out of the car but she barely noticed that as they made their way down the hill, with locals smiling and turning to stare at them, because they stood out like sore thumbs.

Here and there, tourists were browsing, and she knew that they were very likely hotel guests at Niccolo's resort for they hadn't passed another hotel on the way.

'There are one or two bed and breakfast places.' He read her mind. 'But mine is really the only hotel of any substance. The shops are just along here. Pick whatever you want, and if you hesitate I'll be forced to step in and pick stuff for you.'

The boutique was well stocked and catered for rich tourists. It was wonderfully cold inside. It was a shopper's paradise. Ellie stopped point blank in the middle of the large, open space and stared at the rails and rails of rainbow-coloured clothes with dismay. When she turned round, it was to find Niccolo leaning against the wall, arms folded, wry amusement on his face.

'Stuck for choice?' he asked, strolling towards her, which instantly made Ellie take a few steps back.

'I... I...' she stammered, eyes wide, very conscious of the sales assistant who was staring at them with open curiosity.

'Isn't she adorable?' Niccolo looked at the shop assistant and smiled one of those devastating smiles that could make any self-respecting woman jump to his command. 'We're looking for a selection of shorts, swimwear, evening wear...tops...' He looked at Ellie then came a bit closer, to ask in her ear, 'How are you for underwear?'

Ellie looked at him. His face was mere inches away from hers. She could feel his warm breath on her and his fabulous eyes were burning into her skin. 'Not funny,' she spat, and he grinned but didn't step back.

'Okay. But if you don't start choosing, you're going to have to fight off a very keen shop assistant who will want to sell you everything in here.'

She didn't want to. She wasn't mean with her money, but she was frugal. Saving came as second nature to her, with most of her spare cash designated towards paying off her mortgage and putting aside enough to tide her through rainy days. She just didn't *do* crazy spending.

But, as she trailed her fingers along the racks of soft cotton and shimmering voile and silk, a very feminine urge kicked in and she felt a wicked sense of forbidden excitement.

She picked clothes of every hue—shades that resembled the colours of tropical fish and birds of paradise—clothes that she would never have dreamed of wearing in a million years because they weren't sensible.

Memories of her parents in India surfaced, of their hippy friends floating in and out of the beach house they had rented, wearing their gaily painted, flowing, long dresses. There had been a lot of laughter, and that memory took her by surprise, because for a long time her memories of her childhood had been ones of insecurity and unwelcome changes.

Ellie tried on a million things and completely forgot about Niccolo, who had pulled a chair, settled himself in the corner of the room and was on his phone, working.

This was as domestic a sketch as you could get and something fluttered inside her, something scary, because it felt *good* to be here with a man, trying on clothes which someone else would take an interest in, even if it was for all the wrong reasons.

The loneliness of her life struck her like a

forcible blow as she stared in the mirror in the changing room, a vision in orange and russet.

There had been no guy in her life for a long time. What she had seen as being discriminating had sealed all the doors on her personal life and stifled any sense of adventure she could have had.

She didn't want adventure but the colourful, frivolous, silky dress was begging for it. Ellie closed her eyes and, when she opened them again, she felt faint.

She hurriedly stepped back into her sensible clothes, but she had to control her unsteady limbs when she finally presented the stack of items to the shop assistant and stood back as Niccolo settled the bill on his credit card.

'You can have all the clothes back once we've returned to London,' she told him urgently, as once again they were in the sunshine, strolling back up the hill, slowly, because the heat didn't encourage speed.

'What would you suggest I do with all of them?' From behind his sunglasses, he turned to look down at her.

She might spend her time preaching the joys of frugality and the fulfilment of taking the moral high ground, but he'd watched her as she'd become more and more excited at doing something she had very firmly put down. Her tentative selections had become more confident, and Niccolo had to admit that he had enjoyed her gradual enjoyment in succumbing to the very understandable pleasure of shopping for pretty things a lot more than he had ever enjoyed the effusive gratitude he had had from past girlfriends, who had happily accepted his expensive gifts to them as their due.

'I have no idea,' Ellie told him airily. 'But they don't belong to me.'

'In that case, I could always bin them.'

'You wouldn't, would you?' Ellie stopped and stared up at him, and he laughed, warm, genuine laughter that made her breathless.

'I suppose I could have them all dry-cleaned and try and fob them off on one of my sisters,' he drawled. 'But then that would be inviting too much curiosity.'

'What are they like?'

They had fallen into step and the question felt so natural. Not nosy, not prying, just... *natural*.

Niccolo stilled. He realised that this was the sort of conversation he just didn't do. His relationships with women were light and flirty, sexy and seductive, or businesslike and intellectually demanding, but they were never... *personal*. His instinct was to guard his privacy.

'Challenging,' he said shortly.

'Challenging in a good way?' Ellie sensed the shutters dropping but it was hot and sunny and she didn't care about the 'No Trespassing' signs being erected. They had drifted into the market place, which was bustling with people, and she toyed with one of the hand-crafted trinkets at one of the stalls.

'Buy it,' Niccolo said, by way of changing the conversation, and she held it up to the light. It was polished glass, soft and smooth from its life in the sea before the tides had washed it ashore so that it could be made into the necklace she was staring at now.

'This reminds me of...'

'Of what?'

Ellie looked at him and blinked. He hadn't wanted to share any personal details of himself with her. They were on opposite sides of a giant wall and just because they were involved in a crazy charade didn't mean that they were on course to becoming buddies.

'Nothing.' She dropped it back into its hand-made box and spun round on her heels to begin walking quickly towards another stall. A safer one, with fresh fruit and vegetables, but her heart was still hammering inside her at how close she had come to... *To what?*

To thinking that they were more than just work colleagues? Because the sun happened to be shining and the atmosphere happened to be holiday-like?

She was back in control when she turned to find Niccolo walking towards her and she shielded her eyes from the glare, watching him as he approached.

'Time to head back,' he murmured. 'Or you'll end up with sunburn.'

'And that certainly wouldn't be good for business.' She smiled, but her heart was beating fast as they headed towards the car. His hand brushed hers and she resisted flinching at the contact.

'In what way?'

'It wouldn't do for me to be laid up in bed for the week with sunburn when I would need to be out and about, nosing around and getting a feel for the place!'

She stood back as he reached to open the passenger door for her but, instead of stepping aside, Niccolo remained where he was, leaning against the car, sunglasses still firmly in place so that she couldn't read the expression in his eyes.

'On the other hand,' he mused lazily, 'It would probably be just what might be expected…'

'That the naïve English woman would venture out without her sun block and end up resembling a lobster?'

'That the sexy English woman would end up in bed for a week enjoying the ministrations of her man.'

Ellie's mouth fell open and she gaped. The fluttering inside her intensified to become the beating of a thousand frantic wings, and she had a crazy, irresistible desire to moan out loud because her nerves were all over the place, not least because of the way he was staring at her. Just when she thought it was actually safer that he was hiding behind those dark shades, because that way she could pretend that he was joking, he flipped them up with his finger... *He wasn't joking.*

'You don't have to tell me,' Niccolo murmured. 'I can see it written on your face.'

'See what? I have no idea *at all* what you're talking about.'

'Liar.'

'Niccolo...no...'

'I haven't done anything. Yet.'

'This is crazy. *You're my potential client!* I have no idea why we're talking about this!' Her arms should have been pushing him aside, and her legs should have been carrying her resolutely into the car, but instead she hovered, staring dry-mouthed at him.

'Trust me. I'm as mystified as you are.'

'I don't... I'm not... Yes, you're an attractive

man—*as well you know*—but I'm not, *definitely not,* attracted to you!'

'No?'

'No! You're not my type!'

The silence thrummed between them. He was going to kiss her. Her eyelids fluttered. Her whole body was tensed in a state of rigid suspension and a dark, forbidden excitement drummed through her veins until she wanted to pass out. She could almost *feel* the cool touch of his mouth covering hers.

'My mistake, in that case.' Niccolo flipped down the sunglasses and stepped aside. For a few painfully long seconds Ellie couldn't move, then her breathing returned to normal.

Relieved—that was what she should be feeling, she told herself fiercely. She definitely shouldn't be feeling disappointment! She should be *relieved* that he had taken the hint and listened to what she had told him. That he wasn't her type. That it was crazy. She didn't welcome his flirtatious advances! She wasn't attracted to him. Not really…

CHAPTER SEVEN

EQUIPPED WITH HER brand-new wardrobe, the sort of wardrobe to be expected of a woman who was supposedly dating one of the most eligible bachelors on the planet, Ellie decided that she would busy herself doing what she had come to the island to do.

She dreaded the prospect of Niccolo sticking to her like glue. She dreaded the thought of having to wage war with her rebellious body, which was determined to go against all rules and regulations and respond to the wretched man like the girlfriend she most certainly was not.

There were a lot of things she dreaded but, actually, what she discovered she dreaded most was the piercing disappointment when, arriving back at the resort after a silent journey broken only by stilted small talk, Niccolo informed her that he would be busy for the rest of the afternoon and well into the evening.

'Work beckons.' He killed the engine and

leant back against the car door so that he could look at her, his eyes infuriatingly still hidden behind the sunglasses, which left her scrabbling around to try and work out what was going through his head.

'I was about to say that very thing,' Ellie informed him crisply and then pursed her lips together when that remark was greeted with a slow, knowing smile.

'Of course.'

'And I think we should get a few things clear.'

'By all means.'

The grin was still in place, and Ellie bristled, because it just wasn't fair that he could rattle her like this. The heat was gathering in the car now and perspiration was trickling uncomfortably under her stifling outfit.

Sprawled like a lord of the manor against the car door, Niccolo was as cool as a cucumber, perfectly at ease in the soaring temperatures, indeed the very picture of someone unruffled by the electric atmosphere he had deliberately created between them.

He fancied her.

Ellie shivered, tried desperately to shove that horde of buzzing insects back into Pandora's box from which they had come, but her eyes were drawn to the lean beauty of his face, the sensual curve of his mouth, the lazy strength flexed underneath his clothes. He oozed sexy power and the fact that he had pulled back rather than trying to go in for the kill didn't make her want him any less. Rather the opposite. She had protested long and hard about not being attracted to him, but they both knew that those had been empty protests.

She licked her lips nervously, determined not to be undermined by her wayward body.

It had always obeyed the rules! In fact, she had given up on being physically attracted to the opposite sex and had, on countless occasions, told herself that it was for the best because a lack of a love life allowed her to prioritise the things that really mattered, namely her work, her job and moving forward with her career. All those solid things she had lacked growing up.

She was staggered and mystified that it could now choose to ignore all those healthy priorities and behave in ways that made her cringe.

Ellie felt that the holiday atmosphere was partly to blame. She was in the sunshine, surrounded by people who were relaxing, on an island where the pace of life was slow and easy.

Add to that the fact that she had been called upon to play a role that had taken her out of her comfort zone and was it any wonder that she was thinking things that were definitely forbidden?

She realised that she was staring and she cleared her throat with purpose.

'This is an unusual situation,' she began firmly. 'But that doesn't mean that we can't keep our working hats on. Effectively you're my client and, just because we've entered into a pretend charade, doesn't mean that…that…'

'You're stumbling over your words.'

'You can't say those things to me.'

'What things? Clarify.'

'I don't appreciate you talking about any sort of attraction between us. It's highly inappropriate.'

'Really? Because effectively I'm your client? I would never dream of making a nuisance of myself, but neither do I intend to pretend that there isn't something between us.' He shrugged. 'Make of it what you will. Whether I'm your client or not doesn't enter into the equation. The only person I answer to is myself. I'm not someone who has to obey rules in case I get into trouble with someone higher up the pecking order. I'm at the top of the pecking order.'

'That doesn't mean you can do what you like.' Ellie was fascinated by a take on life that was so contrary to her own. To have that much power was staggering. But she knew that, whatever Niccolo said, she was safe with him.

Which gave her no sense of relief because she wasn't sure that she was safe with herself.

Was *he* safe from *her*?

She nearly burst out laughing, because she never thought she would see the day when a question like that might pop into her head. But it had lodged there now and her fists were tightly clenched just in case her fingers decided to wander, her body rigid with tension because so easily she knew it could melt.

Silence settled between them and, since Niccolo showed no sign of dislodging it, it was up to Ellie to say, in a prissy voice, 'So, do I make myself clear?'

'Abundantly.'

'Then stop laughing at me.'

'Was I?' His eyebrows flew up.

'And I wish you'd take those sunglasses off,' Ellie said irritably. 'I'd like to see your face when I'm talking to you.'

'You're beginning to sound like a wife.' He removed the sunglasses and, sure enough, there was humour lurking in the depths of his dark eyes. 'Ellie,' he said softly, his voice a whisper against her skin, bringing her out in goose bumps, 'do you ever relax?'

'Of course I relax!'

'I've never been in the company of a woman more tense than you. Normally, I'm exceptionally good when it comes to making women relax. You're single-handedly destroying my self-confidence.'

Ellie clicked her tongue impatiently but something blossomed inside her, warmed by the lazy teasing in his voice. She'd never experienced anything like it in her life before. 'Please take me seriously,' she half-pleaded and his expression altered.

'I do,' he murmured, intrigued by her obsession with denying the obvious. 'Almost as seriously as you take yourself. Are you always like this, Ellie?'

'Like what?'

'Tightly wound up. You've come over here with a suitcase full of clothes better suited to an office in London. I'm taking it you weren't prepared to let your guard down even for a second. On a tropical island. Surrounded by the ocean and in a six-star resort that has been designed specifically to enable guests to forget all their every-day concerns.'

'I…'

'Yes, I know. You've come here to work and not to enjoy yourself, but—' he shot her a knowing sidelong look '—you enjoyed yourself in that boutique, didn't you?'

'I have no idea what you're talking about.' A guilty flush spread across her cheekbones. He'd looked as though he'd forgotten where he was inside that boutique. He hadn't once looked at the clothes she had been choosing, and he'd certainly not asked her to model any of them for him, even though they had been astronomically expensive, an expense he had borne. One would have thought he would care about where his money was going.

Clearly he'd been watching her, though, and that made her body tingle and burn.

'You kicked up such a fuss, but in the end you enjoyed picking out clothes for yourself, and there's nothing to be ashamed about in that. That was the first and only time I've really seen you relax since we met. You don't have to add to your stress levels by thinking that I won't be able to control my manly urges when I'm around you.' He watched her carefully, amused by the tug of war he sensed coursing through her slight frame, and turned on by it because it was such a novelty. 'If you want to pretend that there's nothing here, then I can't stop you. Or maybe,' he drawled, 'You don't want to pretend that there's nothing here. You just want to ignore it. Which is it?'

Stumped for words, floundering and completely out of her depth in a game of words that felt way too sophisticated for her, Ellie remained silent, waiting to see where the conversation would end up.

'I'm not going to be helpful and join you in that game,' Niccolo said flatly. 'But neither am I going to try and get what you're determined to withhold.' He pushed open the car door and stepped out, pausing to say in passing, 'Shall we meet for drinks later? That'll leave you ample time to circulate. You can contact me on my mobile if you need me.'

'Won't your staff wonder why you're not spending all your spare time entertaining the new woman in your life?' Ellie couldn't resist saying without a degree of sarcasm as she joined him and they began walking towards the hotel.

He wasn't going to allow her to pretend. That declaration of intent rattled inside her head like a beacon warning of danger. They would be sharing a villa and he wasn't going to allow her to pretend that the chemistry between them didn't exist. He was upfront and, unfortunately, not the kind of man easily ignored.

Now that he had opened that box, it wasn't going to be possible to stuff the contents back inside and slam down the lid. Maybe if he had been just another good-looking man she wouldn't have been so flustered. But he had a lethal combination of good looks, humour and incisive intellect that would turn any woman to mush.

He made her think about sex. He made her aware of her body in ways she could never have imagined.

She could feel him looking down at her and she had to stop herself from trembling.

'My staff know me better than to think that I'll be playing tour guide with a woman because I might be going out with her,' Niccolo murmured wryly.

Ellie stopped, shaded her eyes with her hand and gazed up at him. 'By playing *tour guide*,' she said tartly, 'I'm taking it to mean spending quality time with a woman?'

'I spend lots of *quality time* with the women I go out with,' Niccolo asserted with a wolfish grin that left her in no doubt as to the direction of his thoughts.

'I'm not talking about sex,' she said scornfully, pleased, because she was due a timely reminder of just how little respect she had for his take on life.

Sex wasn't love and it wasn't security either. It was a physical, bodily function. Like perspiring, which was what she was doing right now, and she wasn't sure whether it was solely from the heat.

'In that case...' He sighed and laughed softly. 'I would have to say that I spend as much time with a woman as I can given that work, with me, always takes precedence.'

'Always?'

They had fallen into step, with the hotel entrance ahead of them and guests coming and going, some heading out towards the bank of off-road cars exclusively at their disposal, others with towels, heading towards one of the pools.

Some were in pairs, talking quietly, and Ellie wondered whether they were couples who were cultivating a relationship. She still had yet to see anyone under the age of forty.

'Always,' Niccolo drawled.

'You've never been in love?'

He laughed. 'I've had my learning curve,' he heard himself say, much to his surprise. 'Now, unless you want to join me for the remainder of the day, I'm about to head off to see my people and go through a wad of reports.'

Learning curve? What learning curve? Ellie blinked and then, just like that, when she was least expecting it, he dropped a kiss on her lips. A light, barely there kind of kiss. A whisper of a brush, gone before she was even aware it had been there, as fleeting as a snowflake melting before it had the chance to settle.

For the sake of appearances. He was pathological when it came to journalists, as were his guests.

Whatever happened on his resort, he had told her, stayed on his resort. His guests would never fear their private lives being plastered across any tabloids because there had been a pair of zoom lenses observing them from behind bushes.

The sheer scale of the place prohibited that. No lens would be powerful enough to see anything from the outermost borders of the resort which were cleverly manned by all manner of high-tech cameras.

That light, barely there kiss...no one would ever know about it, and for some reason that sent a shiver racing up and down her spine.

But she drew back and looked away, gathering herself, so that when she next spoke her voice was cool and composed.

'That's fine. I'll see you later. I'll make sure I have some thoughts about the campaign, and also about the wider project of promoting the island—if you decide to allow our agency to have the job, of course.'

She nodded crisply and peeled off before she could get involved in another conversation that would leave her feeling vulnerable and confused.

Without having to worry about Niccolo putting in an unexpected appearance, Ellie found that she could really appreciate the resort and enjoy the peace for, contrary to her assumptions, this was no wild match-making resort with irresponsible young things taking advantage of sex on tap.

The place was so vast and the grounds so cleverly landscaped that you could get lost amid the trees and the shrubbery. There were benches here and there, nestled amid the trees, and gazebos and hammocks in unexpected places.

There was ample opportunity to find shade and she knew that this would have been planned out so that no one found themselves with an unexpected case of sunburn.

Somewhere in the heart of the sprawling resort, she bumped into a natural pool carved into the ground. The water was clear, so that you could see that you were swimming with plants and fish, and several guests were relaxing with books and laptops. The only concession to the fact that you weren't totally immersed in nature was the bar area where light snacks and cold drinks were served.

Ellie could see how time could be spent here. So much to explore and, of course, the pace was so lazy that chatting to your fellow holiday makers would come quite naturally.

And everyone was free, single and unattached.

You mingled or chose not to. Somehow, Niccolo and his team had hit upon the perfect formula.

The heat was exhausting, however, and it was a relief to escape back to the air-conditioned villa, where she efficiently jotted down her thoughts. Then, suddenly, it was time to change and the butterflies in her stomach woke up and began fluttering all over the place.

The clothes she had picked earlier had all been unpacked and neatly hung in the wardrobe in her bedroom. In the boutique they had not seemed nearly as alarming as they did now and she stared at the shimmering rainbow-coloured selection in dismay.

But what was the alternative? The starchy greys and navy blues hanging alongside the brightly coloured silks and cottons could have symbolised the struggle taking place inside her, the no-nonsense businesswoman at odds with the blushing girl. Grey versus fuchsia, navy blue versus turquoise.

She opted for a long dress in shades of turquoise and rust with spaghetti straps and the pair of silvery sandals she had bought.

When she stared at her reflection in the mirror, she was looking at a different person.

On impulse, she brushed out her hair. Ever since she had arrived, it had been tied back. Quite sensible, given the temperatures. Now, hanging loose and wavy to her shoulders, she seemed to see all the different shades of chestnut and brown that were always hidden away.

She twisted in front of the mirror and smiled, liking the way everything flowed—the dress, her hair. Her eyes were bright and she had applied just enough make-up still to look natural but...

But different.

She wondered what Niccolo would make of this new Ellie, and she shivered with heady, wicked anticipation as she sashayed her way to the designated meeting point, knowing that, for the very first time in her life, she would be arriving fashionably late.

Niccolo had half-expected to find Ellie waiting for him when he reached the bar area slightly early.

He hadn't glimpsed her once since they'd parted company, but then, that wasn't surprising given the size of the resort.

He expected she would have metaphorically donned her business suit and fought the energy-sapping heat to do her homework and scope out the resort and all its myriad, private little havens which had been specially planned to afford the illusion of being very far removed from the real world.

He had spent the day wondering how much longer they would play this push-pull game of advance and retreat almost as much as he had spent it wondering why he had become so heavily embroiled in pursuing her in the first place.

In between, he had tried to immerse himself in work, but for once his concentration levels had failed him. He'd found his mind wandering.

Sitting nursing a rum and soda, Niccolo half-thought that the clothes she had chosen hours earlier might have been pushed aside in favour of the navy-blue fiascos she had brought with her. The cold light of day had a funny way of killing off all sense of adventure, and she'd been adventurous in that boutique.

Musing on whether she would be armed with her favourite weapon of choice, her tablet, Niccolo glanced up from his drink to see her materialise out of the dark, a vision in blue and orange, and for a few seconds he held his breath.

This was an Ellie he barely recognised and he was transfixed by the vision.

The dress accentuated her slenderness—

the length of her legs, the narrow span of her waist, the pert roundness of her breasts. And her hair was hanging loose, just hitting her shoulders in a thick, colourful mane of waves. As she neared him, he could see that she was wearing make-up. For one incomprehensible moment, he was jealous about the men who might have been looking at her.

He half-stood, belatedly remembering his manners, but she was already taking her seat, composed and in control.

'You shock me,' Niccolo drawled, watching as her heart-shaped face pinkened, although she tilted her chin at a combative angle, prepared to out-stare him.

'Because?'

'I half-expected you to join me in your work clothes to remind me that you're not here to relax or have a good time,' he returned drily.

Ellie opened her mouth to answer that with something suitably sarcastic, but she paused, because…was that really how he saw her? As the dedicated, boring office drone who couldn't operate unless she had a clipboard in one hand and a marker pen in the other? Was that how the *world* saw her? Dull? Reliable? Efficient? The sort of girl who didn't know how to let her hair down and have fun?

He was surprised because, even though she

had spent a huge amount of *his* money buying holiday gear, he had privately thought that she wouldn't really have the guts to pull out all the stops and wear any of it. At least, maybe, not in his company.

She wondered how he would react if she went a step further. What would he do if she took him up on all those suggestive, flirty remarks he had been making? Had he meant any of them, or was it just in his nature to charm, and she the easy bait because he was convinced she would not respond?

What would he do if she responded?

Would he be appalled? Shocked? Horrified?

It would certainly teach him a lesson, Ellie thought with a ripple of recklessness that was quite unlike her. If he thought there was the remotest of chance of her *not* ignoring the chemistry between them, he would probably run a mile.

Her heartbeat quickened. Even *thinking* like that was the equivalent of playing with fire.

'The surroundings are...' She stole a sidelong glance at the intimate semi-darkness of the bar area, with its overhead ceiling fans reminiscent of colonial days, the comfortable bamboo furniture and the wooden balustrade that gave out over the extensive lawns and open land to the front that led down to the coast. 'Seductive.' And she meant it.

Niccolo looked at her narrowly and she held his gaze, only looking away when the waiter approached with a bottle of chilled wine, obviously ordered in advance and with the assumption that she would be drinking.

Which, she decided, she most certainly would be.

'Interesting adjective,' Niccolo mused, sipping the wine and keeping his dark gaze firmly on her face.

His lazy, intimate drawl reminded her of that light-as-a-feather kiss he had earlier delivered and the sudden spurt of recklessness vanished.

What had she been thinking?

'Yet appropriate.' She gulped down a mouthful of wine, suddenly nervous, because, having told herself that those suggestive remarks had been all show and no substance, she found herself wondering whether perhaps they weren't—in which case, what would he do if she responded to them? Where would his hands go? His mouth? She felt faint, and steadied her nerves with another healthy helping of wine.

Watching her, Niccolo wondered whether she was aiming for some Dutch courage and, if so, what she needed the Dutch courage for.

Surely not for one of her work-related conversations? He'd rarely met anyone as incisive as she clearly could be. Some of her observations had been spot on.

'The atmosphere here is seductive.' She cleared her throat and looked around her with an expansive gesture. 'Partly it's the surroundings, but also it's the illusion of privacy.'

'No illusion.'

'You really feel you can relax here without the world watching from the outside—and you're right. I've spoken to a number of the guests here, and that's a big draw for them.' She was back on safe ground. For the duration of the starter and most of the main course, she talked earnestly and non-stop about her ideas for the campaign.

'Of course,' Niccolo interrupted her, as plates were cleared, 'The resort at night is completely different from the resort by day.'

'You mean there *is* night life?'

'More than you can imagine.'

'Where?' Ellie looked around her, took in the full tables and made a mental note of how many of those tables were occupied by couples. She couldn't think where a nightclub might be, but then she'd only seen a fraction of the grounds. Surely, though, music would carry quite some distance in the warm, still night air?

'Probably best if I show you.' Niccolo stood up and waited. The meal had been agony. That one little word 'seductive' coming from her lips had kick-started a series of sexual responses in him that had made the simple process of eating whilst focusing on what she'd been saying practically impossible.

He didn't have it in him to deal with the throbbing, frustrating sexual undercurrent under the surface. Like an over-inflating balloon, it had to be burst, and he intended to do that right now because he wasn't going to spend the rest of his time here trying and failing to concentrate.

'Unless you'd rather stay and have dessert?'

'Do I have a choice?' The wine had done wonderful things for her frayed nerves and the recklessness was back. When, heading outside, he took her hand and linked her fingers through his, she didn't pull her hand away and that had nothing to do with keeping up a charade. In truth, there was almost no need to, as no one seemed to pay them a scrap of attention. The *über*-rich knew how to control their curiosity, probably because they had the curiosity of other people directed at them so often.

They headed for a section of the grounds she had not yet explored. As they walked further along, the sound of the surf became more demanding and then, just when she was about to ask him where they were, the expanse of ocean opened up below them, the dark swell streaked with silver. Here, the waves were bigger and more ferocious, and Niccolo told her that the area was out of bounds unless patrolled by a lifeguard.

Winding, hand-hewn stone steps, lit by fairy lights on the railings on either side, was a magical descent to the bay on which the enormous waves pounded against rocks in the ocean and close to the shore.

'The night life,' Niccolo murmured softly.

He had led her towards one of the craggy rocks that littered the beach, which was so different from the icing-sugar sandy beaches that enclosed the resort.

Ellie looked at him as he leant against the perpendicular face of the black rock. The moon picked out the lean, stunning angles of his face and there was something so achingly beautiful about his dark beauty, about the way he was staring off into the distance, that she longed to reach out and touch him.

She longed to break her rules just this once.

'There's something musical about the sound of the sea, wouldn't you agree?' Niccolo looked down at her to catch her staring at him, her mouth parted. 'A dramatic orchestra of sound, with crescendos, lulls and rising tempos.'

'Are you secretly a romantic?' She breathed and Niccolo laughed shortly.

'Please don't delude yourself into thinking that,' he said drily. 'This resort aims to give the punters what they want and need without even being aware of it. Picture-postcard beauty is one thing, but sometimes something more elemental can be just what the doctor ordered.'

Ellie didn't believe him. 'You must feel *something* when you stand here.' She took a couple of steps towards the surging black sea, and Niccolo instinctively reached out to hold her back, which made her feel warm and squirmy inside. 'Not just,' she said breathlessly, 'Pragmatic because it might appeal to the guests.'

Niccolo shrugged, instinctively pulling back, because habit had shaped him into a man who didn't share.

'I don't do romance,' he informed her in clipped tones. 'So, if you're leading me into a place where you think an outpouring of touchy-feely emotion is going to take over, then you're barking up the wrong tree.'

Ellie saw the flash of white teeth as he backed away from a contentious topic to grin at her. 'Now,' he drawled, 'If you're *really* interested in hearing how this rugged setting makes me feel, then I'm very happy to elaborate, but I'll bet you might end up squirming because it goes against your high-minded principles.'

'Tell me.' The words were out and she wasn't even tempted to take them back.

She sensed his stillness and recognised that she had crossed a line. *One night.* Would that be so very bad? Maybe he would laugh and turn her away, but at last she would find out, and wouldn't end up being the coward who would look back and wonder 'what if?' for ever...

'Where are you going with this?' Niccolo questioned coolly.

Ellie knew that the shutters were falling fast and she was gripped by a sudden desperation to take a chance.

'You were right,' she said huskily. 'About the chemistry. It's there. Well, it is for me, anyway. Maybe you've just been playing games because there are no other distractions around to grab your attention.'

'I already told you, I don't do games.' Niccolo didn't move a muscle. 'Life's too short. But you don't do *sex without strings*, or have you forgotten all about that?'

'I haven't forgotten.' Her voice hitched on a note of fervent earnestness. 'But you confuse me. You make me question things I never questioned before.'

Niccolo wasn't into soul-baring but he found that he was holding his breath and not swiftly trying to change the subject onto more familiar ground.

Ellie reached out and ran her finger along his muscled forearm and, when he stiffened in immediate response, she was suffused with a sense of soaring triumph.

'I'm careful.' She took her time sifting through her thoughts to find the right words, but feeling vulnerable to be confiding like this in a man who clearly didn't welcome confidences. 'Maybe too careful. And I may disapprove of relationships based on sex, but I would never allow myself to let sex morph into a relationship.' Ellie wondered if she was making herself clear. She certainly was to herself. She was making perfect sense to herself.

There would be no happy-ever-afters with Niccolo Rossi, but she wouldn't be looking for any. She would retain control over the situation because she was making a conscious choice.

It wasn't a choice she had ever thought she'd make, because she'd always been rational when it came to sifting her way through the confusing tangle of relationships, but this was a chemistry against which she had no weapons. It wasn't weak to succumb. On the contrary, it was strong. She was proving to herself that passion wasn't necessarily dangerous, just so long as you didn't confuse it with love, and that would be a lesson that would stand her in good stead.

The boyfriends she had had in the past had ticked all the boxes but the one marked passion, and she could see now that passion was something she couldn't shove into the background as insignificant.

Accepting that made her feel empowered. She wasn't stepping out of her comfort zone. She was broadening her territory.

This was what it felt like to be totally in charge of life around you. Instead of shying away from danger, she was nullifying the danger by taking it head-on, eyes wide open. And not just *taking it on,* but *enjoying it.*

'I'm making a choice,' she said, then she shrugged just in case he started thinking that she might be trying to pin him down, just in case he needed an exit. 'The rest is up to you.'

CHAPTER EIGHT

ELLIE DIDN'T KNOW what to expect. For what felt like an agonisingly long time she held her breath, conscious that this was the most daring thing she had ever done in her whole life.

She'd become so accustomed to playing it safe. How had that happened? she wondered. How had she allowed the years to roll by without daring to test the waters? Why had she always assumed that because you got close to the fire you would end up being burned, when in fact you might just end up feeling warm and enjoying the warmth before walking away from it, no harm done?

His kiss was soft, exploring, a meeting of mouths, a twining of tongues, and she melted into it as if it was the most natural thing in the world.

She shuffled towards him, wrapped her arms around his waist and stood on tiptoe to reach up to him as he reached down to her. His tongue probed and darted, and she moaned softly. The shimmering, soft fabric blew against her legs.

The layers of clothes separating them were no barrier against his desire. It was a powerful indicator of just how turned on he was by her.

Daringly, Ellie ran a trembling hand over the bulge distorting his trousers and Niccolo deepened the intensity of his kiss, moving from tender to demanding, giving her no time to surface.

'Romantic setting,' he broke off to say in a husky, uneven voice, 'but not exactly practical for what I have in mind.' Niccolo was shocked at the uneven tenor of his voice. This was *not* the lazy, teasing, confident voice of someone in control of his responses. This was the voice of a horny adolescent on a date with the hottest girl in the school. Well, he hadn't been that horny adolescent for a long time and he breathed in deeply, regaining control.

'I knew you found it romantic here,' Ellie murmured with a husky laugh. She stared up at him and he glanced away briefly, but then looked back down at her with a wry smile.

'It's romantic,' he conceded. 'Will you be putting that in your mock-ups?'

'This whole resort is romantic. I'm spoilt for choice.'

'Yet there are no nubile young things leaping behind bushes so that they can rip one another's clothes off.'

'No, not much leaping behind bushes,' Ellie agreed.

'Not unless you count us.'

'Niccolo...'

'Is an "on second thoughts" conversation looming? Or are you about to tack *Take me, please* to the end of my name?' Niccolo prided himself on being able to walk away from any woman because there was no woman tempting enough ever to make him seriously lose his head. Granted, he had never been in the position of actually thinking that he might have to walk away from one before he got his fill, but the uncomfortable thought now occurred to him, and he didn't know what to do with it. Not cool.

'I'm not having second thoughts.'

Relief rushed through him with the force of a tsunami. 'In that case, yes, of course I'll take you. Back to the villa and straight into my bed.'

The heat in his voice made her shiver. She was so hot for him that she wanted to tell him to shut up, to just *take her*, right here and right now, and hang the discomfort.

Instead, she said in a rush, 'I've never done this before.'

'I know.'

'You know?'

'You've spent long enough telling me how much you disapprove of chance encounters that lead to sex. I've got the message, Ellie.' He nuzzled the satiny smoothness of her neck and she whimpered and melted a little bit more. 'You've never done sex without the promise of a relationship, even if the relationship didn't work out in the end. So choosing to have scintillating sex with me on a tropical island with nothing at the end of it but a wave goodbye is a first for you. Don't worry, my darling, I promise you that you won't live to regret your decision.'

Niccolo very slowly drew up the silky, long dress, scooping it until the soft fabric fell over his big hand, until he could feel the warm nakedness of her skin underneath, the brush of her thigh.

Ellie opened her mouth but her words were lost in a cascade of sensation as he expertly curved his hand between her legs to caress her inner thigh, his knuckles nudging her, scraping against the thin material of her underwear.

She couldn't think when he was doing this. She certainly couldn't hold down a sensible conversation about the embarrassing truth of her virginity.

Thoughts flashed through her mind, darting like quicksilver. She tried to picture his reaction if he knew that she'd never actually gone the full distance and slept with a guy. Amusement? Horror? Would he take it in his stride? Or would he run for the hills? Ellie doubted that virginity would appeal to a man like Niccolo Rossi. 'Virgin' and 'casual sex' were two things that didn't go together. Moreover, what if he didn't want the bother of having sex with someone who didn't know the ropes?

Having dared, Ellie didn't know what she would do if Niccolo decided, for whatever reason, that he didn't want to take on the responsibility of having sex with a virgin. Now that she had come this far, she *had* to go the whole way. *She had to.*

Which meant that she wouldn't say anything.

Not difficult, bearing in mind that her vocal cords had dried up under the devastating impact those caresses were having on her.

'I can tell how much you want me and I like that. A lot,' he said huskily. 'You're ready. Shall I see how ready?' He slipped his hand under her knickers, a shockingly intimate invasion that made her gasp, but there was no time for her to draw back because her whole body was besieged by sensations she had never experienced before.

This was what craving felt like. This feeling of *wanting* that was so powerful it made your whole body shake from the force of it. If molten lava had poured from the open heavens she wouldn't have been aware of it, because all she was aware of was the pressure of his finger against her body, teasing it until she wanted to scream and beg and plead.

When he withdrew that exploring finger and gently arranged her knickers back into position, she could have wept with frustration.

'You're stopping. Don't stop.'

'You won't thank me after if we make love on the sand.' Niccolo could also have said that he was doing himself a favour in stopping because he was so turned on he felt like he would explode unless he took a step back.

He'd barely laid a finger on her! It was crazy.

Hands linked, they couldn't make it to their villa fast enough. Time to reflect. Time to think about what she was about to do. *Time to change her mind.*

Ellie knew that this was a valuable break in proceedings. It would take them fifteen minutes to get to their villa. Longer, if they were stopped *en route* by guests or staff members. Niccolo was ridiculously popular. He could barely walk ten metres without someone wanting to have a chat about nothing in particular.

During that time, there would be ample opportunity for her to stand back and look at what she was doing under the glaring, cold light of reality.

Nothing of the sort occurred. If anything, the frustration that had shot to the surface when he had removed that deliciously questing finger from inside her only ratcheted up, up and up so that she was squirming by the time they were finally back at the villa.

The air was balmy. The roar of the ocean had faded to an insistent, soothing, background sound, replaced by the harmonious orchestra of night insects—frogs, toads, crickets and grasshoppers.

Niccolo pushed open the door to the villa and swung her inside all in one fluid motion, then he swivelled so that she was against the closed door, then he kissed her. And this wasn't the exploring, lazy kiss of before. This kiss was hungry, urgent, demanding...wanting what was on offer.

Pressed with her back against the door, Ellie reached up and wound her arms around his neck, pulling him down to her.

She was desperate for his finger to be back

where it had been and she wriggled as he kissed her.

'Don't be impatient,' Niccolo broke away to tell her with a grin in his voice. 'I'm not going to rush this. I want to touch every part of you and I want to take my time.'

'Niccolo…'

'Here is slightly more preferable to the beach but not as good as my king-sized bed.' He lifted her off her feet as though she weighed nothing, and Ellie gasped and then laughed as he took the steps up two at a time, kicking open a bedroom door but not bothering to turn on any lights.

Not that there was a need because the bright, silver moon poured sufficient light through the window to illuminate a bedroom that was slightly bigger than hers and just as exquisitely furnished.

He carried her to his bed and gently deposited her, then he stood back, head tilted to one side, feasting his eyes on her rumpled sexiness and wondering what it was about her that he found so compelling.

Her hair spilled about her face and her dress was hiked up to the thigh. It gave him a delicious kick to acknowledge that she hadn't done the predictable thing and tugged it back into the interminably modest mode. But then she was stepping out of her comfort zone. He couldn't wait to see where that took them.

He watched her intently as he removed his shirt. Half-naked, he waited a few seconds, drinking in her slumberous, greedy gaze.

He removed his trousers and tossed them aside. Her eyes widened.

From her prone position on his bed, Ellie absorbed the enormity of what she was about to do with rapidly beating heart. She'd never wanted anything more, but apprehension at the physical act made her breathless and giddy.

He was so beautiful. Like an exquisitely carved Greek god brought to vibrant life. His shoulders were broad and muscled, his chest, with its dark, curling hair, tapered to a wash-board-hard stomach and a narrow waist.

'Relax,' Niccolo murmured, slipping onto the bed next to her, then flipping her onto her side so that they were face to face, looking at one another. 'You're as skittish as a colt.' He found her naked thigh with his hand and smoothed his palm over it. 'Your skin is like satin,' he murmured. 'Has anyone ever told you that?'

'No,' Ellie answered truthfully. Her voice was shaky.

'Why are you so nervous? There's no need to be. Trust me. You're going to enjoy every second of being out of your comfort zone. Who knows…you may never want to return back to it. Shall I continue doing what I was doing on the beach? Hmm? Would you like me to touch you down there until you're squirming against my finger?'

'Niccolo…' Ellie said brokenly, legs opening of their own accord, body shifting into just the right position for his hand to settle over her feminine mound.

She moaned and stilled, arching a little as he slid that devastating finger over her until she was panting, until her attack of nerves was lost under the weight of mindless sensation.

Desperate for the feel of skin against skin, Ellie wriggled up to hook her fingers under the hem of the dress, yanking, tugging and then abandoning the effort because Niccolo seemed to be so much better when it came to clothes removal.

The sultry breeze through the open windows caressed her suddenly naked skin. Ellie could barely open her eyes, but open them she did, to see him removing the last vestige of his clothing. Boxers joined trousers in a heap on the ground somewhere.

He was impressively built. From a position of absolutely no experience, Ellie recognised that much. Straddling him, she felt a roar of excitement race through her, and she circled him with her hand and then hitched up so that she could trace a delicate line around his girth with her tongue.

Niccolo reared back and groaned, fingers curling into her hair so that he could press her to take him in her mouth.

Tasting him was heaven. She wriggled a bit more so that she was on her knees, in just her underwear, bent so that she could devote all her attention to him.

The outer reaches of her daredevil, abandoned wantonness astounded her. Where on earth had it come from?

She fell back as he gently tugged her away from him and sighed with pleasure as he removed her bra and underwear.

'You're good at this, aren't you?' Ellie moaned, conjuring up a marching parade of the blonde supermodels who would have preceded her.

'Very good,' Niccolo assured her, without a trace of false modesty. 'Now, keep quiet and enjoy. And relax...'

He'd fantasised about her breasts but no fantasy could have done justice to their pert roundness, to the deep pink discs of her nipples. He lowered his head and attended to the pressing need of tasting them. He drew one into his mouth, sucked hard on it, licked its stiffened tip with his tongue until he felt her squirm. Her skittishness had gone, as he had known it would. By the time he was ready to enter her, she would be hot, wild and desperate.

But that time wasn't yet, however out of control he felt, and however fast and hard he wanted to take her without any further foreplay.

He wanted to savour what he'd waited for and, frankly, what he'd pursued, contrary to all his natural inclinations.

He worked his way down from her breasts, felt the rise and fall of her chest as she sucked in oxygen in deep, moaning gasps.

He circled her belly button with his tongue and then, winding his way yet lower, pushing apart her legs wide enough to accommodate his body between them, he sensed her tense.

It was something that impinged on his consciousness for a matter of mere seconds.

He was way too submerged in his own delicious loss of self-control and the urgent pounding of his runaway libido to pay attention to what was happening on the outer fringes of his consciousness.

Niccolo lowered his mouth to her. She smelled of honeyed musk. A deep, hoarse groan greeted the explorations of his tongue.

Her legs widened and she pushed up, her whole body stiffening and then bucking as he delved deeper and licked harder and faster.

At this point, experience had taught him that the game of proving expertise would commence. Women liked showing him what they could do. Some form of gymnastics was usually involved. They would do their utmost to demonstrate their prowess between the sheets in the hope that they might hold his attention for longer than their predecessors.

Not this time. This was pure, undiluted enjoyment and he thought that a man could get addicted to it.

Ellie wasn't trying to prove anything to him. She was just luxuriating in the pleasure he was giving her with his hands and his mouth. Niccolo didn't want it to end.

He knew when her orgasm was building, and he knew how to gently ease her away from it, and he was amused that she didn't even bother trying to conceal her anguished frustration.

Only when he reared up to reach for the condoms in his wallet on the bedside cabinet did he once again sense a hesitation.

'Niccolo…' Ellie paused but then closed her eyes and smiled, too turned on to care about any long speeches about virginity, high moral principles and the importance of love.

'Needs must.' Niccolo misread the soft tremor in her voice. 'I'm a man who never takes chances.'

An experienced man, Ellie thought. *A man who thinks ahead and plans ahead and controls every aspect of his life.*

Except he was about to make love to a woman who had never been there before and she was sure that would give him pause for thought. If not more than that.

Ellie didn't think he would guess because she was so ready for him.

She was wrong. He thrust into her, a fierce, deep thrust, and she cried out, body stiffening in automatic rejection of something she had, deep down, been apprehensive about.

Niccolo stopped immediately. For a few seconds, he was confused. Had he hurt her? He was big. He knew that. But there had never been a woman who hadn't stretched to accommodate his girth, who hadn't, indeed, revelled in the feel of his hard shaft inside her.

Then he understood, and he immediately eased himself out of her.

'Why didn't you tell me?' he asked quietly, tilting her so that she had no option but to look at him.

Ellie licked her lips and glared at him with defiance. 'Tell you what?'

'That you're a virgin.'

'Because I knew you'd burst out laughing.'

'Am I laughing now?'

'Because,' Ellie admitted with painful honestly, 'I'd made my mind up to sleep with you. I'd made a choice I'd never come close to making at any time in my life before and I thought that if you knew that…if I told you that…well, you'd run away.' She looked at him sullenly, breath held.

'Why would you think that?'

'Because you'd get spooked, Niccolo. You'd start thinking that I might become one of those clingy women who start thinking there's more going on than there really is—one of those boring nuisances who get over-involved and refuse to let you do the decent thing and ditch them without a backward glance.'

Niccolo flushed darkly. 'Whoever said that I was like that?'

'No one has to,' Ellie told him kindly, regaining some of her humour, and relieved that the elephant in the room was out in the open and he hadn't, as she'd thought, grabbed his belongings and run for dear life.

'So you think you know me, do you?' Niccolo said softly. 'You come with a very large suitcase stuffed full of preconceptions, Ms Eleanor Wilson. If I recall, you thought you had a handle on what my resort was going to be like. A squalid, steamy meeting point where rich, idle, young, unprincipled things could have casual sex. You also reckoned that you were far too principled to ever indulge in sex unless a full-fledged relationship was on the table...'

'My principles are still intact.' She stroked the side of his face. 'I made a conscious choice. If I'd decided to stay away from you, then we wouldn't be doing this. In fact, we could be lying naked on a bed together and I would be able to stay away from you.'

'Is that a fact?' Niccolo drawled.

'Fact.'

'I don't believe you.'

'That's because you have an ego the size of this villa.'

'That small?' Niccolo loosed a warm, teasing laugh. 'Disappointing. I always thought it was a lot larger than that.'

Ellie glowed. Niccolo had a point, hadn't he? She'd found it easy to put things into boxes. Life was easier that way. No nasty surprises. What had started out as a defence mechanism had more or less become a way of life. She was on her own because, somewhere along the line, she had failed to see that within those boxes there was room for all sorts of permutations.

It didn't mean that the integrity of the box had to be compromised.

Yes, she'd come to the resort with a certain image in her head. And, yes, she had pigeon-holed a man who was turning out to be more than just sexy and rich. Niccolo Rossi, she was finding, had all sorts of complexities she'd never expected. His sense of humour was one of them.

'And here's where you've made another mistake,' Niccolo murmured. 'I'm not scared off because you're a virgin.'

'You're not?'

'I'm honoured that you have chosen me,' he told her seriously.

'And you're not scared that I'm suddenly going to do something stupid?'

'Like fall in love with me?' Niccolo laughed. 'No. No, I'm not. We're both alike insofar as we know the boundaries of this game. Neither of us came here looking for anything. Anything found us. But I'm no more suited to you than, as you've pointed out on a thousand occasions, you're suited to me. This will be our adventure while we're here in paradise.'

'And once we've left?'

'Life goes on.'

Sex for the sake of sex. Anathema to her

very soul. But the siren call of adventure was irresistible.

It made sense in this new world of hers, where the parameters had shifted and grey areas had been allowed to blend with the black and white ones.

Besides, cutting to the chase, did she have a choice? The man was temptation personified.

'Trust me,' Niccolo murmured. 'I'll be gentle.'

He talked as he slowly eased himself into her. He felt her relax and her excitement made it easy. Nerves had got the better of her but the nerves were gone and it was almost as though he knew her body as well as he knew his own.

He pushed deeper, felt her tightness and thrilled to the soft moan that escaped her lips, but he waited until she wanted him to move faster and harder, waited until she could no longer bear the restraint.

For Ellie, nothing had ever felt so good. Sensations raced through her, lightning-quick, splintering through her body and carrying her up, up and up on a rising crescendo of unbearable pleasure. For the first time in her life, she had shaken off the shackles of caution and common sense and she felt wonderfully *alive*.

This wasn't the Eleanor Wilson she was accustomed to being, the Eleanor Wilson who had a wardrobe full of sober suits and buttons-to-the-neck blouses for every possible work occasion. This wasn't the Eleanor Wilson who clicked her tongue with impatience when she listened to her parents telling her that she should have a little fun before it was too late. This Eleanor Wilson took risks and *liked it*.

But risks came with health warnings, didn't they?

Through the glorious waves of pleasure swamping her, that barely audible voice of common sense tried to make itself heard, but Ellie firmly squashed it and succumbed to the heights to which she was being blissfully carried.

His controlled thrusts had her arching and groaning, writhing as he moved deep inside her.

She climaxed with explosive force, shuddering against him and clinging to him so that her fingers dug into the taut muscles of his shoulder blades. When she cried out, it was as though she was hearing the guttural cries of someone else, not her.

Through slumberous eyes, she watched as Niccolo climaxed on a single forceful thrust, his big body rearing up and tensing. He was a thing of beauty, whether he was cool and composed or sexy and teasing or, like now, hot, sweaty and in the throes of passion.

'That was *so* good.' He breathed huskily, easing himself off her and disposing of the condom before turning onto his side so that he was looking at her.

'Are you sure?'

'Any regrets?' Post-coital conversation was somewhat foreign terrain for Niccolo. He'd never made a conscious effort to avoid after-sex chit chat. It was just something that had never really happened. It was as though, once the physical lust had been sated, he'd become filled with an urgent restlessness to get up, get showered and carry on with the more pressing demands of work which were never very far away.

This, he acknowledged, was an unusual situation and, as such, required an unusual response. He decided that it was a mark of him, as a man, that he could rise to the occasion and not fall in line with his natural inclination to get out of bed and have a shower.

'None.' Ellie looked at him earnestly. In the moonlight, his eyes glinted and the angles of his beautiful face were blurry. His body, lightly touching hers, was having a dramatic effect, turning her on even though she was sore from penetration. 'I'm glad we made love.'

She sighed. 'I wouldn't say my virginity has been an albatross round my neck, but I realise that I should have just been far more relaxed about sex and accepted that physical chemistry can exist in isolation from everything else that matters.'

She tried and failed to think back to any time at all in her past when she had struggled to resist the sort of elemental, overpowering *need* that Niccolo had roused in her. She frowned. Surely there must have been at least *one* guy who had caught her eye? Made her think twice about her dearly held principles? *One bad boy?*

'You sound as though you've read that noble statement in a book somewhere,' Niccolo said drily. 'But, good. I'm glad you have no regrets. Nor do I.' He shot her a wolfish smile that made her toes curl. When he smoothed his hand along her thigh, she quivered in sensual reaction.

If this was the power of lust, then the power lay conclusively in his hands, Ellie thought with a twinge of dismay. He'd done something to her from the very moment she had first laid eyes on him in that gym. Being in his company, seeing first-hand all those sides of him that made him so dangerously three-dimensional, had compounded the spell he had managed to weave over her. Not only was she not thinking straight, she wasn't thinking at all, and that scared her.

Niccolo was surprised to discover that having her once wasn't nearly enough. He was raring to go again. 'If you're not up to another bout of love-making, then I know myriad ways we can pleasure one another without penetration.' He nuzzled the slender, pale column of her neck and lightly covered her breast with his hand. Ever so gently, he rolled his thumb over her nipple, teasing it until it was stiff and erect. 'I could taste every succulent inch of your body and then you can come against my mouth. How does that sound? Hmm?'

Too good, Ellie thought, backing away, because somehow, somewhere in the dim recesses of her desire-addled brain, she knew that if she attached herself willingly to the noose he was tossing round her neck then he would be able to take her where he wanted. That was just the way he was. She would become another mesmerised clone and it would be goodbye to the free-thinking, outspoken woman who had somehow ended up in bed with him.

Against reason.

Yes, she had chosen to end up bed with him, but no, she wasn't going to choose to allow him to dictate the pace of whatever passing flirtation was going on here.

In the heat of the moment, she'd barely given passing thought to the fact that, once they were off this island, they would probably see each other in the course of work. It was be Niccolo's worst nightmare—to have indulged in a few days of heady passion only to find himself trapped into having occasional dealings with her because of work commitments.

Well, she wasn't going to give him cause to think that he would have to start taking evasive measures because she might become a pest.

'It sounds wonderful.' Ellie firmly removed his hand from her breast and tucked it where it belonged, which was anywhere but on her body. 'But I'm going to have to pass up on that tempting offer.'

Niccolo's eyebrows flew up and he looked at her in astonishment.

'Where are you going?' he growled as she slipped her legs over the side of the bed.

'Back to my bedroom, of course.' She glanced at him over her shoulder and smiled sweetly. 'I'm really tired. It's been great, but I think I should get a good night's sleep if I'm to be of any use tomorrow. I mean, I'm here to do a job, after all.'

CHAPTER NINE

'WHERE ARE WE GOING?'

This as Ellie jumped into the four-wheel drive, twisting to look at Niccolo as he slid into the driver's seat.

After only just under a week on the island, he was darker than he had been, his lean, hard body a burnished gold. He bore no resemblance to the urbane, sophisticated be-suited businessman who strode through the corridors of power in London like the king of the jungle. He was in a pair of loose, khaki shorts and a faded, striped tee shirt and he was no longer meticulous with his shaving. Right now, at a little after two in the afternoon, faint stubble shadowed his jawline. He looked breathtakingly sexy. She had an overwhelming urge to reach out and stroke the side of his face or his arm, but gestures like that felt *too* intimate.

When she had left his bedroom five days ago, she had set a standard that had to be maintained. The standard was she kept a bright and cheery smile on her face and gave no inkling that what had begun as an adventure was turning into something a lot more serious for her.

She didn't quite know when the line had been crossed. She kept telling herself that it *hadn't* been crossed, that she *was* still enjoying a random sexual encounter, and the reason she was so affected by it was because it was so out of the ordinary.

That was what she told herself, but in the early hours of the morning a little voice in her head told a different story.

She had feelings for him. Somehow, they had crept in through the cracks and taken over her head and her heart. She still stuck to her guns and slept in her own bed every night, but she would desperately have liked to stay in his, woken to him in the morning, felt the freedom of reaching out to touch his body and having him turn to her with sleepy arousal so that he could take her.

The end of this little bubble in which they had taken refuge loomed on the horizon like gathering storm clouds on a sunny day. The days and nights had reached their conclusion.

'It's a surprise,' Niccolo drawled.

Ellie laughed nervously and he slanted her a sideways glance and smiled. 'Don't look so nervous. I'm hoping you'll be pleased with it. You deserve a nice surprise, Ms Eleanor Wilson. We leave the island tomorrow and you've done a first-rate job.'

'There wasn't much to do. The place lends itself to superlatives. I've started putting together some ideas for the brochure you want to distribute alongside the advertising platform. I think you'll be pleased.'

Niccolo's lips thinned. She was talking work. That was *his* thing. Work was paramount and always had been. However, he had to fight down a feeling of irritation that the very one thing he should be relieved she was still focusing on got on his nerves.

When he took her to bed she was the most abandoned, passionate creature he had ever slept with. He couldn't get enough of her. But when they weren't between the sheets, she reverted to type, always reminding him that she was there, first and foremost, to do a job.

'A man could almost feel used,' he had joked, although there was an undercurrent of truth there that really wound him up because, for the first time in his life, there was an element of uncertainty that made him feel like he was walking on shifting sands.

He didn't like it.

But it didn't make him want her any the less.

'Are you going to launch into a slide-show presentation?' he asked with a sarcastic edge.

Ellie ground her teeth together. She dearly wanted to tell him that it was all right for him—sex, for him, was just a physical act to be enjoyed. For her, there had been a seismic change, and talking about work was her way of clinging to normality. Without that lifeline, a parallel universe opened up in front of her that was frankly terrifying. It was one in which she ended up devastated because she had fallen in love with him.

Her brain skidded to a halt and her breathing quickened as she desperately tried to reject that appalling notion.

'I haven't got the equipment,' she said lightly, staring out of the window and closing her eyes as the breeze blew her hair in scattered strands across her face. 'Tell me where we're going.'

He laughed, that sexy, husky laugh that always sent little chills of pure pleasure racing up and down her spine, and the awkward moment and all her unsettling thoughts were set aside. They drove away from the compound and town to a part of the island she hadn't yet visited. A new batch of guests was due to arrive in a couple of hours, Niccolo was telling her, so he intended her to have time out before then and he knew just the spot.

The vehicle followed a dirt path and then bumped its way to a rough siding that gave out onto a beach.

It was perfectly empty, except for a boat dragged onto the sand and tethered to a tree.

'We're going out to sea.' He killed the engine and turned to her.

'You know how to handle a boat?' Ellie breathed.

'When are you going to start realising that I know everything?'

'You're so egotistic, Niccolo.'

He had fetched towels from the back of the car and was leading the way towards the boat which was a basic little contraption with an outboard motor, a simple shelter and bench seats. It was nothing like the sort of boat she would have pictured him enjoying, and she said so as he detached the boat and pushed it out into the calm-as-a-lake turquoise sea, holding her hand as they waded in the shallow water and hopped on board.

'Sometimes simple is good,' he murmured, striking out into the great blue ocean on a sea that was as still and as smooth as glass.

'You've told me that you never eat in.' Ellie slid a glance across to him and gazed at his perfectly chiselled profile as he stared out to the open sea from behind his dark sunglasses, one hand resting lightly on the wheel, the other on the rudder. 'People who like simple things enjoy eating in.'

'If I'm on my own,' Niccolo drawled, 'I'm either working, in which case I eat the nearest thing that happens to fall into my hand, or else a member of my family has decided to take me under her wing and feed me up. If I'm with a woman, we eat out. I like the atmosphere of a restaurant. It's not conducive to thoughts of domesticity.'

'Why are you so apprehensive about the concept of domesticity?'

'Why the question-and-answer session?'

'Forget I asked.' Ellie shrugged, hurt because it had been a simple question and he had rebuffed her without bothering to try and paper over his abruptness.

'Tell me about your family.' She changed the subject, moving to neutral territory. 'You never talk about them.' Not, she thought guiltily, that she had volunteered any information about hers. She shuddered to think what he would make of her eccentric, hippy parents with their allotment, their crystal-and-gem shop and their free-spirited liberalism. Not that he had asked.

She was curious about him but the curiosity was obviously not mutual.

'There's nothing extraordinary to recount,' Niccolo returned mildly. 'I have three sisters and a mother.'

'That's why you're so comfortable in the company of women,' Ellie mused. 'I've seen the way you chat to all the women at the resort, from your staff to the guests. You have a talent for putting them at ease.'

'I had no idea you were analysing me,' Niccolo drawled. He looked at her, his expression suddenly closed and thoughtful. 'That could be a dangerous pastime.'

'Why?'

'Any woman who sees me as a project is destined to failure. What you see, Ellie, is what you get. Good sex.' His sensual mouth curved into a smile of satisfaction. 'Very good sex.'

Ellie reddened. *Message received loud and clear,* she thought. 'I wasn't analysing you,' she told him lightly. 'That's your ego talking, Niccolo. I was just expressing curiosity. Believe it or not, a bit of curiosity about the man you're sleeping with really isn't that unusual. I certainly don't see you as a *project.*' She laughed and looked away, squinting at the impossibly blue ocean in which their little boat was an insignificant splinter of glue and wood. A puff of wind and the rise of a wave, and the splinter of wood would be gone, just like that. 'The only man I will ever see as a project will be the man I want to settle down with.

'Spotted any suitable candidates at the resort?' Niccolo kept his voice light. He'd noticed a couple of the guests looking at her. The sun and the sea, not to mention the hot sex, had turned the nine-to-five working girl into a sun-kissed, sexy little number. Her brown hair had gone curly in the heat and the scattering of freckles across the bridge of her nose made her look years younger.

'How could I?' Ellie laughed, relaxing as the boat chugged its way further and further out into the wide blue yonder. 'Aren't you supposed to be the love of my life?'

'Is that the charade we're pulling off?' Niccolo wasn't looking at her as he said this. 'I thought we were a little more casual than that.'

Ellie kept smiling. Her jaw ached from the effort. 'At any rate, if I'm supposed to only have eyes for you, isn't it going to look a little fishy if they're checking out the guests?'

'You're telling me that you haven't seen any potential soul-mate candidates? There are some very eligible guys here.'

'Are you encouraging me to have a look?' Ellie asked lightly, stung, even though she didn't know why she should be because he was just being honest with her. 'What would you do if someone took my fancy?'

'You're a free agent.' Niccolo shrugged. 'What could I do?'

He was unsettled by the flare of raw jealousy that ripped through him when he thought about her sizing up one of the men at the hotel. They were all decent guys, and she deserved a decent guy, but he still didn't like the thought of her finding someone she wanted to play footsie with under the table before taking him home to her mother.

He didn't do jealousy. In fact, it was an emotion that left him cold, and he shifted uncomfortably, relieved that his destination was within sight. He slowed the engine.

'Well, I haven't, not that the men I've chatted to haven't been lovely guys. I actually feel sorry for a couple of them. They may have stacks of money, but they don't seem to have an awful lot of confidence when it comes to the opposite sex, which is why they're still single I expect. They all have stories to tell. I hadn't expected stories. I was wrong about that. They could use a few lessons from you when it comes to confidence with the opposite sex.'

'I don't think I'd be the right example,' Niccolo said wryly. They had arrived at a vast, shallow pool in the middle of the ocean, where the extraordinary formation of coral had created an oasis of warm, calm water that glittered with rainbow-coloured fish visible from the boat.

'Why not?' Ellie murmured absently, leaning over the side of the boat, captivated by the spectacle. The sun was very hot, beating down on her shoulders. She had worn a loose tee shirt, something she had picked up from the well-stocked gift shop at the hotel, and a pair of linen shorts and she itched to remove both so that she could get down to her bikini.

Both hands resting on the side of the boat as she peered into the clear, calm water, trying to play 'spot the fish', she felt the boat dip then the feel of Niccolo's arms looped round her waist. Instinctively, she straightened with a sigh of pleasure, twisting round so that she was looking up at him.

Niccolo flicked off his sunglasses and their eyes tangled. 'Because,' he murmured, confusing her for a few seconds, because he was picking up on the observation she had forgotten making, 'I may know how to talk to the opposite sex, but the men here aren't looking for ways of making successful small talk. They're looking at ways of connecting on a slightly more permanent basis and, when it comes to that, I'm no good on the advice front.'

'Is this your way of warning me off?' Ellie didn't look away.

'Do you need warning off?'

'Of course I don't. I know what this is about. You don't have to worry that, because I joked about the guests at the hotel thinking that we're in love, I meant it. You asked me if I'd seen anyone here I could picture myself being with and, if I were to answer you seriously, then I would tell you that I haven't. The men here are nice, and they certainly don't fit the mould when it comes to what I'd imagined, but they're not for me.'

'Not young enough?'

'I'm not ageist, Niccolo. I just don't go for the whole money thing. It's not how I was brought up. This thing between us… Well, it's fun and it's really made me look at my choices in a different light—and for that I'll always thank you—but you needn't worry that I'm going to start confusing gratitude with anything else.'

'You're going to return to playing it safe now that you've had your walk on the wild side?'

'That's right,' Ellie said lightly.

'I expect Mummy and Daddy will be pleased,' Niccolo murmured, trying to picture what form *safe* came in. Glasses? Short back and sides? Shirt and tie, even when relaxing? He'd never been the safe sort in his entire life. You didn't get to the top by playing safe and he'd wanted and needed to get to the top.

He'd had to. He'd had his path mapped out from he'd been young. He'd known his responsibilities—to make sure his mother and his sisters were taken care of. He'd given his word to his father as a child.

Niccolo frowned, because this was the first time he had thought about his father in a long time. Where had that come from?

Ellie grinned, keen to get away from the jagged edge to their conversation and to return to the easy, teasing familiarity they had developed over the past few days, almost communicating without words.

'They'll be bitterly disappointed,' she told him, breaking her own personal vow to keep things light—and 'light' didn't include confiding any more for her than for him. But she couldn't help herself.

'Really? Explain.' Niccolo perched on the side of the boat which bobbed on the calm blue water. The only sound was of the sea lapping gently against the side of the boat.

He had undone the buttons of his shirt, which hung open, offering a tantalising glimpse of hard, bronzed skin with its speckling of dark hair. Without thinking, she stepped forward and rested the palm of her hand against his chest. Niccolo instantly took it and kissed the soft underside of her wrist, eyes fixed on her face as he teased the sensitive spot with the tip of his tongue.

'You were saying?' he encouraged. 'Keep talking. Don't mind me.'

'Give me back my hand and I'll keep talking,' Ellie said breathlessly.

'I'm afraid I can't do that. Now that I've captured it, you're going to have to relinquish it for at least another fifteen minutes. Just long enough for you to tell me why your parents would be disappointed with the crashing bore you intend to bring home to them.'

Ellie laughed. They were back to normal. She could postpone the uncomfortable issues lurking on the edges of her consciousness and enjoy the moment.

'I like routine because it's something I never had,' she confessed, closing the tiny distance between them and resting her head against his chest, which was hot from the sun. She glanced up at him with a faraway expression.

'My parents didn't lead a very ordinary life,' she said with a touch of exasperated affection in her voice. 'They liked to think of themselves as *travellers*, as in the hippy variety. Lots of moving from one country to another and getting wrapped up in all sorts of spiritual soul searching and Zen Buddhism. And lots of smoking pot and inviting fellow hippy travellers to stay wherever they happened to be. Or else, we stayed with them. It was always a muddle.'

She sneaked a glance to see whether there was disgust on his face, because her life couldn't have been further from his, but he was looking at her with a guarded, non-judgemental expression.

'You need to be rooted to one spot,' Niccolo mused pensively. 'You like knowing where you are and you don't like change.'

'Now who's the one doing the analysing?'

Niccolo laughed with a touch of irony. Analysing women was something no one could ever accuse him of doing, but she was right.

'But, yes, that's about the size of it.'

'Hence your taste in men. Most women would think it extraordinary to list *boring* as a desirable trait in a man, but you're coming from a different place.'

'Reliable doesn't have to mean *boring*,' Ellie protested, laughing.

Niccolo couldn't see the joke. 'But it usually does,' he pointed out with cool logic. 'Men who don't take chances usually find their comfort zone in the slow lane.'

'That's not fair.' She tugged free of him and stood back, eyes as cool as his, wondering how they had progressed from warmth to shade in such a short space of time. 'You just don't understand because you come from a completely different background to me.' She was beginning to wish she hadn't said anything. He had never asked for confidences and it was clear he didn't welcome them.

'Everyone has their story. You said you'd seen that with the clientele here. Not just a bunch of men and women looking for cheap thrills but living, breathing human beings searching for something they might or might not find. You think my background has somehow shaped me into being ambitious?'

'More than just ambitious.'

'I've had to be. You had your wandering parents who taught you what it was like to yearn for routine. I learned from childhood how lonely it could be trying to be a man when you haven't even started shaving yet.'

'What do you mean?'

'I was left in charge of my family, sworn to look after them, at an age when I could scarcely look after myself. I gave my word to my dying father and I said goodbye to my childhood the instant that oath left my lips.' He was shocked at his confession. 'And I have no idea why I just told you that. We were talking about safe men. What I should have said is that I'm a man, and I know what men are like, and safe men are dull. They're the paper pushers without whom no business could function but they're also the ones whose names are easily forgotten.'

'A paper pusher would suit me fine.' But there was no heat in her voice. She desperately wanted to ask him more about his childhood, to cling to that fleeting confidence and hold onto to it, but knowing that every shutter within him would drop if she were foolhardy enough to try and quiz him further. 'Not everyone wants a dynamo!'

'But dynamos are so good in bed,' Niccolo murmured, his voice changing from cool to sexily husky. He pulled her towards him and kept holding her. He'd confided and that had been a mistake. This was what he should have done because it was what he was good at. Sex. Without giving her a chance to answer the unanswerable, he undid the button of her shorts, and then the zip, and he shoved them down in one easy motion. 'And out of bed as well.'

'Niccolo, we're having a conversation.'

'You're missing the scenery.'

'Where are we?' Ellie reluctantly dumped the conversation, even though she felt as though she still had points to make about what he had said.

'In the middle of the ocean. An anomaly here means that the water is very shallow and very, very warm. And full of marine life. It's a bit like stepping into fish soup.' He was talking and kissing her neck at the same time, and she squirmed, looking past his shoulder.

'We can swim here?'

'Of course we can. Why do you think I brought you? Swim and make love.'

'Niccolo…'

'Shh.' He had moved her bikini bottoms to one side for access and his finger explored her lazily, thoroughly, with a teasing rhythm that made her gasp. 'Take your top off,' he commanded. 'We're shaded here. You should be safe from the sun.'

'What if someone comes?'

'Trust me, there will be ample advance warning. Outboard motors aren't silent.'

It felt wickedly, wonderfully decadent to take all her clothes off out in the open, with the cool breeze taking the edge off the hot sun and with ocean all around them.

Niccolo groaned and cupped her breasts. He played with her nipples while the ache between her legs begged to be relieved. She touched herself as he continued to kiss her and knew that he was smiling at her abandon.

Very gently, he sat her on one of the smooth, worn wooden benches that ran the width of the boat. The craft was small but it was far from shabby. Propping herself upright on her hands, face upturned, mouth parted, eyes shut, she felt him nudge her legs apart, and then she melted as he began licking between them, taking his time, in no hurry at all.

The sound of his mouth against her matched the soft sound of the water lapping against the side of the craft. Ellie felt the muscles in her groin tighten, and she gasped sharply as waves of pleasure began building. She wanted him in her so badly but she wasn't going to make it.

Her orgasm came with explosive force, her fingers curled into his hair, her body heaving and rocking until she was spent.

Then she watched as Niccolo removed his clothes, her sated body awakening all over again in record time. Out here, in the middle of the ocean, there was no concept of time. Maybe this was what eternity would feel like, Ellie thought dreamily. She wished she could bottle the feeling and then she would be able to hold on to it for ever...

* * *

It was dusk by the time they returned to the resort. The day had been wonderful. Ellie hadn't wanted any of it to end. They had swum, made love and returned to the beach for a picnic tea, which she hadn't even known he'd got the restaurant to prepare for them.

The hours had gone past in a haze of lazy contentment.

And that was what love felt like.

Ellie wasn't going to fight it any longer nor was she going to try and pretend that it was something else.

An adventure...a learning curve...a daring experiment...lust...

When she'd told him that she was a virgin, he'd replied that she could trust him because he wouldn't hurt her. She was going to be hurt but she knew that, given the chance, she would do it all over again.

She began opening her door as he killed the engine but he stayed her with one hand.

'Enjoyed today? Even though you were wary of the surprise I had in store?'

She grinned. Night was falling and his face was in shadow. 'It couldn't have been better.'

'Would a safe lover have taken you there, do you think? You might discover that if you seek out safety you find a guy you end up scorning, because there's no adventure without risk.' Niccolo hadn't planned to return to this conversation but something inside him drove him, like the ferocious urge to pick away at a scab.

'Maybe you're safer than you imagine,' Ellie murmured. 'Maybe we're more alike than you think, both of us too cautious to really let go when it comes to relationships.'

Niccolo was uneasily aware that this was a conversation he had to pilot. 'Which is why this has worked between us. Neither of us is inclined to be persuaded into thinking that there is anything more to what we have than sex. We're both realistic and sharp enough to see the pitfalls.'

'But I do believe in love,' Ellie said with heartfelt sincerity.

It just doesn't happen the way you sometimes plan it happening. It just sometimes ambushes you, and by the time you find out it's too late to do anything about it.

'You don't. Even though you have this—a fantastic six-star resort designed for Cupid's bows and arrows?' There was genuine curiosity in her voice.

'This was, first and foremost, a business proposition. Long story, but let's just say that I was more than fifty percent certain that it had wings before I started laying the first brick.'

'It's all about business with you, isn't it, Niccolo? What did she do to you?'

Niccolo looked at her narrowly. 'Come again?'

'Forget it.'

He should. Instead, to his astonishment, he said with acid bite, 'I made one mistake many years ago. I misjudged a woman. The person I thought she was was a chimera, an illusion, smoke and mirrors. If ever there was a single event to focus my mind and remind me of my purpose in life, it's that youthful mistake.'

And so his life, Ellie thought, had closed in for ever. The boy had become the man who had locked his emotions away and thrown away the key. She glanced at his lean, handsome face and was chilled to the bone. Yet something about his brooding, closed expression made her want to soothe him, and she fought the urge, dragging the conversation back to the present, pre-empting his retreat.

'We all have our demons, don't we?' she murmured. 'Hopefully some of the people here will find their other halves who are happy to share their demons. This place was just made for love and romance. It's so, so beautiful. Definite brochure material.'

She was in love with him and, now that she had faced that reality, she could understand why she had fallen. There was so much to him, so many sides, so many complexities. No one would ever come close to matching him and that was something she would have to accept. But…he had just shared with her and she feverishly wondered if that meant anything.

She couldn't help herself. Her brain veered off at a tangent as she tried to analyse whether that door that had opened, through which she had been allowed a peep at a side of him he hadn't shared with anyone, meant anything.

One batch of guests had left, or most of them. Several had, indeed, left with promises to meet in the outside world. Cupid had landed a few arrows. Now, with the lights of the resort twinkling around them, Ellie could see a new lot of guests gathering, awkwardly making polite conversation.

The group numbered about twenty. Most were in the same age bracket as the group that had just departed—middle-aged men and women in search of a dream, or else happy for companionship with a member of the opposite sex.

But there were slightly more younger people, and one in particular stood out because she was taller than the rest, with the bold, dramatic looks of a catwalk model.

She was peering around her through slanted

eyes. Her blonde hair cascaded down her shoulders in a poker-straight sheet, as smooth as silk. Her clothes, Ellie noted, were as impractical as hers had been when she had first arrived on the island, but for different reasons. Whilst Ellie had come equipped for business meetings, the blonde model had come equipped for man-eating. Her dress was ridiculously tight and ridiculously short and her heels were ludicrously high—stilettoes that catapulted her to over six feet. Next to her was an expensive-looking suitcase and a smaller, matching pull-along.

The blonde made eye contact with them and the flash of instant recognition was not, Ellie knew, for her. That flash of recognition was for Niccolo, who had stopped dead in his tracks.

Ellie felt his stillness and went cold.

'Friend of yours?' she joked, but her voice was high pitched and falsely cheerful.

'I know the woman, yes,' Niccolo answered, without glancing down at Ellie.

Ellie's heart clenched. She had wondered about the women he'd dated and now she knew. Women with the sort of looks that could eclipse most mere mortals. Women who garnered second and third stares, and accepted grovelling attention from men as their rightful due.

The woman in question was sashaying towards them, each leggy stride sexy, undulating and unhurried. She scooped the blonde hair back with one hand and shoved the mane over a shoulder. She was beginning to smile as she focused on Niccolo with every ounce of her attention.

Ellie had been rendered invisible and, the closer the woman got to them, the more invisible she felt. She had shrunk to the size of a matchstick by the time the blonde was standing in front of them, with eyes only for Niccolo.

'I hoped I'd find you here, Nicky,' she purred. 'I couldn't believe it when I was told that you were holed up on some island in the middle of nowhere, but it all made sense when I found out that you actually practically *owned* the damn thing!'

'Amy, I'd like you to meet Eleanor. Eleanor, this is Amy Carter. We knew one another a while ago.'

'Nine months, darling. Hardly *a while ago*.' She smiled, curled her fingers into the neck of his shirt and tugged him playfully towards her. Then she squinted down at Ellie and stared at her with cold blue eyes for a few seconds. 'Darling...' She tilted her head to one side to flash Niccolo a meltingly beautiful smile. 'Would you mind terribly skipping off so that Nicky and I can have a little chat?'

Ellie's mouth dropped open. *Skipping off?* Had she suddenly turned into the hired help, told what to do by one of the guests?

'I… I…'

Her brain screamed, *Who the heck do you think you are? Get lost!* Her mouth, however, was opening and shutting like a stranded goldfish and nothing was coming out.

'Would you mind, Ellie?' Niccolo finally looked at her with a shuttered expression. 'I won't be long.'

CHAPTER TEN

THERE WAS ONE thing Ellie was not going to do—she was *not* going to kick up a jealous fuss. She was *not* going to give any indication that she had spent an hour and a half fuming and imagining all sorts of things. She definitely was *not* going to utter those immortal words of a dyed-in-the-wool harridan: *What time do you call this...?*

But she couldn't busy herself in her bedroom pretending that nothing was wrong. She was sitting upright in one of the wicker chairs in the airy sitting room when Niccolo finally made it back to the villa.

'You're back,' she said, turning as he pushed open the door and entered the room, moving to pour himself a whisky and soda from the built in-bar that was restocked on a daily basis with every imaginable drink and plentiful supplies of ice.

Niccolo paused and looked at her with

a thoughtful expression. 'Did you think I wouldn't be?'

Ellie reddened and tilted her head defiantly. 'Who knows?' She hated the shrill, cutting edge to her voice. 'Gorgeous blonde ex appears out of nowhere, sends me *skipping off* on my way and that's the last I see of you for nearly two hours! On our last evening here.'

With a future that was as hazy as summer mist because nothing had been discussed. Things had been shared, hopes raised, but it felt like a mirage. *And now this.*

Niccolo's lips thinned and he spun round on his heels and poured his drink without saying a word.

Then he remained where he was, leaning against the bar, feet loosely crossed at the ankles.

Was it any wonder jealousy was tearing her apart? Ellie thought miserably. He was just so unfairly sexy, and to be pursued and cornered here by a woman who could stop a bus in its tracks with her superb good looks, looks that matched his... Well, what man wouldn't stand back, look at the plain Jane he had been sleeping with and do the predictable comparisons?

Of course, she'd known what she'd fallen in love with. She'd fallen for a guy who was out of her league. Too rich, too good-looking, too powerful, too…*everything*. Forget about the fact that they weren't suited to one another on a fundamental level. On a superficial level, they were chalk and cheese, but while they'd been here she had been able to kid herself that there was a connection.

The leggy blonde bombshell had thrown that all into perspective and it was like having a jagged-edged knife plunged into the core of her.

Ellie could have dealt with picking up the pieces in the quiet of her little life back in London. She would have fantasised that, even if they hadn't ended up together, it was because he was a commitment-phobe and not because there hadn't been a real connection.

He'd opened up to her, hadn't he?

But the blonde had stripped her of that illusion and shown their brief affair for what it was—the attraction felt by a man who could have anyone towards the one woman who had put up a fight. Even though the fight hadn't exactly lasted very long.

'I won't be explaining myself to you,' he said coolly, 'If that's where this hissy fit is going.'

'I am *not* throwing a hissy fit!'

'No?' he drawled, sipping the drink and looking at her impassively over the rim of the glass. 'Well, you're certainly giving an excellent impression of doing that. Hissy fits turn me off.'

Ellie gazed at him helplessly and he stared back at her in complete silence until she looked away. She was shaking. She sat on her hands while the blood rushed through her, hot and furious, bringing her out in a fine film of perspiration.

'I warned you not to get attached,' he told her, voice calm, even and dispassionate, although inside a stab of guilt was making the pulse in his temple throb.

She looked so damned young, sitting there like a chastised school kid, as fresh and as innocently sweet as the ex he had just dispatched had been hard and anything but innocently sweet.

This was his fault. He should never have gone there. But he had been greedy for an experience that promised to satisfy his jaded palate and then, when he should have stopped, he had continued because the enjoyment had been addictive.

He should have listened to the warning bells which had started ringing from the very first words she had uttered—all that romantic clap trap about soul mates and happy-ever-afters—and had culminated in her admission that she had never slept with anyone before.

And then, he had told her things he had never told anyone else and he still couldn't fathom what had possessed him.

'I couldn't help it.' Ellie didn't bother with the pointless charade of pretending that she had no idea what he was going on about. She lifted clear eyes to his. 'I never meant to get emotionally involved, but I won't deny that I have, which is why I'm here—' she smiled sadly '—behaving like the sort of person I hoped I'd never be.'

Niccolo drained his glass. He could have told her that he had sent the ex back to London on his private jet without even giving her time to unpack her bags. He could have told her that Amy Carter was a bunny boiler and he had blessed the day he'd booted her out of his life nine months ago. But he was in a dangerous place and placating her did not strike him as the best of ideas.

Of course, things would have to end between them, and something twisted inside. He clenched his teeth together, suddenly in need of another stiff drink.

'Have you eaten?' he asked politely. 'I'm afraid I won't be able to have dinner with you. I've ignored pressing work concerns and I feel that I might use the rest of the evening to remind myself that I have a job to do. Tomorrow reality is going to make its appearance and I have several reports that have been languishing untouched.'

Emotions chased each other on her face, hurt giving way to comprehension, giving way to quiet acceptance. Each was a further twist of guilt inside him because *he* had caused those emotions. He'd been selfish and arrogant and, never having been one to explain or justify his behaviour, was feeling what it was like to want to explain and justify his behaviour.

The less dialogue, however, the better. He didn't want to initiate any kind of conversation that might encourage her to think that there was something there that could be cultivated against all odds.

There was nothing.

Niccolo hit a wall of bleakness, which was new and unsettling. He had always accepted that his priorities were not the priorities of other men. Of course, he enjoyed the company of women, but he wasn't cut out for love, not the kind of love that most women craved. Not the kind of love that Ms Eleanor Wilson craved and deserved.

It wasn't just because he'd had one bad experience. Most people recovered from a bad experience. For the first time in his life, Niccolo considered the train of events that had moulded him into the man he had turned out to be. He was at the top of the pecking order when it came to money and success but when it came to emotional fulfilment—the sort of fulfilment he saw in his two married sisters— well, that was something he had always accepted he would never have, and had been rather pleased with himself for being able to intellectualise that reality. No kidding himself, just honest acceptance of fact.

He'd messed up big time once and wasn't going to repeat the mistake, but also…

Ellie had made him think of his father, had made him remember those words spoken when he had just been a kid, that promise made to take care of his family, to be *the man of the house.* He had adhered to that oath and had never been released from it.

For better or for worse. It was a marriage of sorts when you thought about it.

He smiled wryly. This was how he was and he was never going to change.

'Of course,' Ellie said, banking down the tears and smiling at him, 'I'm sorry I fell for you. You were very fair and gave me sufficient warnings. But I'm not unhappy that I did and I'll be fine.'

'Good.' He hovered. He didn't want to leave her, and he decided that that was understandable, because only a callous bastard would have been able to turn his back on her without a twinge of conscience.

'There's a chance I might have to travel to Hong Kong sooner than expected, so you won't be dealing with me in all likelihood when your pitch is completed. And, for your information, the job is yours. I'll get my person to email your agency with the formalities.' He forced himself to sever all ties. A clean break, no backward glances.

'Yes,' Ellie said politely. 'I understand. I'll be able to get the entire package across to you by the end of next week. Would that be okay?'

'That would be fine.' Niccolo tilted his head to one side and glowered at her with brooding intensity.

But in the end, Ellie was the one to leave the room, walking past him with her head held high and only collapsing when she was in her bedroom, back pressed against the closed door, eyes squeezed tightly shut against a future that stretched out ahead of her like a never-ending, black void.

Ellie eyed the suitcase standing in the middle of the room and stifled a sob of misery.

It was astounding to think that a handful of days, during which her life had been changed for ever, lay in that little suitcase. A collection of floaty, rainbow-coloured tropical garments which she had brought back with her three weeks ago. She hadn't had the heart to bin the lot because they had cost a small fortune, but neither was she going to keep any of them, so she had had them all cleaned, had packed them into the suitcase she had travelled out with and now here was that suitcase, ready and waiting to be taken to one of the charity shops on the high street.

She would drop it off on the way to visit her parents. There was no rush for her to get back to London because there was no job for her to return to. Sleeping with Niccolo had not only opened a door to heartbreak but had kick-started a domino effect in her life that had culminated in her breaking away from the agency she had helped to build. Her partners had agreed to buy her out, though they'd both been sorry to dissolve their partnership. Her last day had been on Friday and that was that. For the first time, her life had become an un-ravelling ball of string, and she didn't know how or where to start to gather back up the strands so that she could turn them into some-thing halfway recognisable as *her life*.

For once, she couldn't wait to see her par-ents. They would sweep her up, ply her with cups of herbal tea and her mother would press a few crystals on her and tell her all about their healing properties.

For once, Ellie would not be judgemental, because she had discovered, to her cost, that training your life to follow the path laid down by common sense and practicality was not always possible. Control had a way of slipping away and for the first time Ellie could understand how that happened. She knew that she could never be the free spirit her parents had been in their youth but neither was she the buttoned up, blinkered woman she had trained herself to be. Not any more.

Time and again since Niccolo had walked away from her, she had told herself that that was a good thing. She just actually had to start believing it, because right now all she wanted to do was curl up and abandon herself to memories of Niccolo and what they had shared.

She had given up on hearing from him. She'd known that he wasn't going to get in touch but, still, she'd *hoped*. Hoped that he'd read those ugly headlines that had been splashed across the tabloids, waiting for her when she got back to London—*billionaire struck by Cupid's arrow on his own Love Island*. Except the humiliating truth was very far removed from that. He'd dodged the arrow which had whistled right past him and embedded itself into *her*. She'd told him how she felt. She'd wanted him so badly just to give them a chance, and she'd just kept on hoping that at some point he'd have a rethink and get in touch.

Heading into the bedroom for a last-minute check, and also to fetch the bag she had packed to take to her parents, Ellie made a monumental effort to look forward and not back. She had something quick to eat and then she was off, and when she returned to her little house one door would be shut and hopefully she would be able to see another one opening.

'What do you mean, she doesn't work there any more?'

This was the first time Niccolo had actually involved himself in the advertising campaign for his hotel in a number of weeks. In fact, ever since he had left the island, leaving behind a sleeping ex-lover tucked up in her own bed and catching a series of connecting flights that had delivered him halfway across the world.

He had felt like a cad doing his disappearing act but it had been for the best. *He* would have been able to handle the enforced proximity of both of them being in the villa on that last day, but *she* most certainly would not. She had invested in him and he knew that his continuing presence would have been an unsettling source of unhappiness for her. So he had done the decent thing and removed himself from the situation, ordering his own jet to return from where it had dropped Amy back in London to collect Ellie.

But he'd still felt like a cad.

Clean break, he had told himself, burying himself in a series of high-level business dealings, first in Hong Kong, then in Australia.

Phoning to find out how she was doing didn't come under the heading of 'clean break'.

Some vague nonsense had hit his ears, thanks to his sisters, about their brief fling becoming public knowledge thanks to Amy—who had returned to London and promptly got her own back, it would seem, by telling a scandal-hungry gossip column about the affair between him and Ellie. Niccolo had very firmly sat on that and told his nosy siblings that they could stop trying to press him for details about something that no longer existed.

If he'd winced when he'd said that, it was only to be expected, given how things had ended between himself and Ellie.

It was frustrating that work had not done what it should have done. He hadn't been able to focus and, the harder he'd tried to nail down why he was still thinking of her, the more frustrated he had become.

Which, in turn, had made him stubbornly remain out of the country for longer than originally intended.

But now he was back. In the end, he'd had no choice. Need, desire and much, much more had won an unequal fight. He'd stayed away for as long as humanly possible but then, two days ago, details of the campaign had been emailed to him and he'd buckled under the force of his memories.

Every sentence, every picture, every poetic description had been the story of their romance. Because a romance was what it had been, even if he hadn't seen it at the time. He'd flicked through her draft and had seen her lovely face, heard her infectious laugh, felt himself long to touch her slender body. He'd immersed himself in what she had written as thoughts for the brochure he had mentioned, and he had been taken back in time to something he should never, ever have let go.

Now here he was but where the heck was *she*? He felt sick with a surge of sudden apprehension.

'She…er…' Marta, one of his execs, glanced over to the guy in charge of marketing in the little team set up to handle the venture.

'Well?' Niccolo growled impatiently. 'Spit it out!' He'd barely touched down a few hours ago but his body was suddenly revving up, as though suddenly put onto high alert.

'Well after all the business of…of…'

Thick silence descended and Niccolo frowned. 'Business of what?'

'Apparently,' Marta said, tiptoeing around the subject with agonising delicateness, 'After the…er…situation between you two… I guess… I mean, it's only a guess…'

'She no longer works for the firm,' Paul interjected abruptly. 'But, sir, all the information has been handed over to her colleague and that's all that matters.'

'No. It's not.'

She'd been kicked out of the partnership. He'd had his fling with her and she'd paid the ultimate price—and the guilt that had been sitting on his shoulders attacked with full force. His sister had told him that it had been in the gossip column, but he had made sure to avoid reading any of it, so he had no idea what, exactly, had been written.

'I'll deal with this later.' He was already heading for the door, contacting his PA for Ellie's address, and for the first time in weeks feeling a certain amount of peace.

He hit the ground running. From office to

car and car to street was accomplished in under five minutes, and then he was on his way to find out what the heck was going on.

Ellie heard the sharp buzz of the doorbell with a groan of despair. She was on her way out! She'd endured an uncomfortable week of intrusive reporters popping up in all sorts of places to ask questions but that had died off. The world was full of scandal, and after a short while there were more pressing ones to write about. Married celebrities caught with their clothes off in bed with their wife's best friend had more mileage than a single guy, however rich, having a fling with a single girl, however poor.

The few friends she had made over the years had been far more curious, but now Ellie thought that there was nothing left to be said on the subject of her folly and she had no idea who could have their inconsiderate finger glued to her doorbell.

She opened the door hesitantly, keeping the chain on, and then fell back, heart pounding.

The last person she expected was Niccolo but there he was, as impossibly handsome as she remembered, without a suit jacket or tie and with the sleeves of his shirt cuffed to the elbows.

Dark, dangerous and still so painfully irresistible that all Ellie wanted to do was reach out and touch.

Instead, she remained where she was without unfastening the chain and stared at him. 'What are you doing here?' she asked eventually, when it looked as though the silence was going to last for ever.

'You're no longer a partner at the agency,' Niccolo said gruffly. He raked his fingers through his hair, glanced away, then back to her, his body vibrating with restless energy.

Ellie looked down. 'No. It seemed best,' she muttered.

'Did they ask you to step down? Because of *us*? If that's the case, then they can say goodbye to my account, and goodbye to any future in London, because I'll make sure they become lepers of the advertising industry. They may not know who they're dealing with. I will remind them.'

Ellie sighed. 'Maybe you should come in,' she offered reluctantly. She didn't want this. How was she supposed to get over him if he was in her house? She remembered her confession to him, her proud declaration that she had broken all the rules he'd laid down and fallen for him, and inwardly she cringed.

She could deal with that humiliating memory when she was on her own but, now that he was here, it resurfaced like a bad dream.

She knew that he was staring at her as she led the way into her small sitting room, before turning awkwardly to offer him something to drink. Tea, coffee...

'I can't be long,' she said stiltedly, when both had been refused. 'I'm leaving London for a while.'

'What happened?' Niccolo demanded.

Leaving London? To go where? London was her comfort zone, her security blanket. Where was she taking herself off to?

Guilt struck him with the force of a sledge-hammer. He had been able to brush off pesky rumours because things like that had no effect on him. At the top of the food chain, Niccolo Rossi could do as he liked. But it wasn't the same for her. He thought of her vulnerability and wanted to groan out loud.

She'd told him that she had feelings for him and he'd run faster than a speeding bullet. In fact, he'd run so fast and so far, he'd ended up on the other side of the world. He'd left her wounded and to her own devices to face the consequences of an affair he had instigated.

If she had feelings for him then, she would hate him now, because his behaviour had been appalling.

A sense of urgency gripped him, along with a dreadful fear that he'd left everything way too late.

'Where are you going?' he asked tersely, and Ellie folded her arms and looked at him, cool and composed, because she'd had her moment of opening up to him once upon a time and she wasn't going to be going down that road again.

'To stay with my parents,' she said bluntly. 'Not that it's any of your business, Niccolo. And, if you've come because you somehow feel responsible for the fact that I no longer have a job, then there really is no need. What happened between us, happened. Yes, there was fallout for me, but nothing I can't deal with.'

'This is my fault.' Niccolo didn't know where to begin. Guilt was not something he had ever had use for. For once in his life he was at a loss as to how to find the right words for what he knew he had to say.

'I don't think so,' Ellie said coolly. 'We both did what we did with our eyes wide open. I'm not about to take the coward's way out and start playing a blame game.'

'Did they ask you to leave?'

Ellie flushed. 'They didn't,' she said heavily, 'Because you're so important that it doesn't matter what you did. If I'd made the mistake of sleeping with someone in middle management, then I'm sure things might have been different. Yes, I was a partner, so I wouldn't have been kicked out, but I would have felt compelled to hand in my resignation. I dissolved the partnership of my own free volition. Happy now? They were generous in buying me out. I will have enough for life to carry on until I find something else. Somewhere else.'

'Tell me what happened. Leave nothing out.'

'Niccolo,' Ellie groaned, angry with him for showing up and angry with herself for not having got over him half as much as she'd thought she had. 'What's the point? I don't want you here!'

'Please, Ellie. I...' He raked his fingers through his hair and shuffled his feet.

He looked hesitant, and she was so astounded by that that she lost some of her fire. In its place was a dreadful exhaustion at the direction her life had gone in. And yet, she knew, she would have it no other way, because her life before, so well ordered and so well worked out, seemed like an empty shell in retrospect.

'You what? Feel sorry for me? Think you should at least offer me a consoling pat on the back because I'm out of a job? Feel guilty? Want to placate your conscience by making sure I'm not about to jump off the nearest bridge?'

'None of those things.'

'Then what?' she muttered with simmering hostility.

'I've been...' Niccolo hesitated, on the brink of revealing his vulnerability, which was just the sort of pathetic weakness he had never had time for. 'I've been out of sorts,' he conceded awkwardly. 'Since we broke up.'

'Poor old you.'

'I've missed you,' he told her in a roughened undertone.

Ellie looked down and clenched her teeth because there was no way she was going to be dragged back into something that was bad for her because of any stupid seeds of hope that might spring into existence on the back of honeyed words.

'Tough,' she gritted, with a conviction she was far from feeling.

'If I've blown it...' Niccolo breathed heavily '...then tell me right now. I'll leave and you'll never see me again if that's the case.'

'Blown what?'

'My chances with you.'

'You don't have any chances with me. I'm not going to be hopping back into your bed because you've missed having sex with me.'

'I would never ask you to do that.'

'Then do you mind telling me what it is you're asking?' Ellie was so tense that her body was on the brink of breaking into pieces. She forced her leaden legs to take her to the sofa where she collapsed in a grateful heap, tucking her legs under her and keeping her arms folded as she did her utmost to outstare him.

'You miss the sex,' she muttered, 'But you could have sex with any woman you wanted. I could see from that other woman's hungry expression that she wanted to eat you up. You threw her aside and she's still so desperate that she followed you all the way out to that island so that she could try and reconnect with you. So if you're missing the sex now, then give it a few weeks and you'll soon find a suitable replacement.'

She felt the same painful tug of searing jealousy that had fired her up at the villa and sent him fleeing to the other side of the world in panic. She had become the proverbial possessive nag and she was being one now. It was in her voice.

Although, he wasn't running. In fact, he wasn't breaking eye contact, and she glared at him resentfully.

'I missed more than the sex,' Niccolo finally confessed. He'd found his way to the sofa and was sitting right next to her, leaning in to her, his big, powerful body doing all sorts of things to her equilibrium.

'No, Niccolo,' Ellie sighed wearily, 'You don't. Sex is what you do, and it's *all* you do, and if I hadn't got the message loud and clear then I certainly had it rammed home to me when you fled the scene of the crime after I told you how I felt about you. I've never seen anyone run so fast in the opposite direction.'

'I know I ran,' Niccolo admitted quietly. 'But what did you expect?'

'Nothing more.' Ellie gritted her teeth. She wished he would just back away because she was pressed up hard against the arm of the sofa with nowhere left to go unless she stood up but she feared her wobbly legs might just give the game away.

'And I know why. Amy showed up out of the blue, and when you reacted the way you did I panicked.' He flushed darkly. 'My life had become complicated the minute I jettisoned all my self-control and gave in to the temptation to have you. It didn't make sense, and it wasn't like me, but I couldn't stop myself. Something about you appealed to me from the very second I saw you and I couldn't get what it was. It was…frightening.'

Ellie looked at him from lowered eyes, not

wanting to listen and start believing anything he said, but unable to resist the pull of his words. She thought back to the range of sensations that had assailed her when she had first seen him in the gym, and reluctantly understood what he was trying to say, because it had been the same for her.

Against all odds and everything she believed in, she had been attracted to him from the start, and had been as helpless against the force of that raw, chemical attraction as a lone swimmer trying to fight the drag of a raging undertow.

'So?' she threw at him.

'You're not going to make this easy for me, are you?'

'Make *what* easy?'

'The fact that I'm doing my best to tell you that I was an idiot.'

'For running away when you weren't through with me?'

'Don't, Ellie,' Niccolo said roughly. When he ran his fingers through his hair, he was startled to find that they were shaking. He never got nervous, but he was nervous now. Thing was, he couldn't blame her for attacking him. At least she hadn't frogmarched him to the door, and that was a blessing he had every intention of taking advantage of.

'For not realising that, instead of running away, I should have been hanging on to you for dear life because it just so happened that you were the best thing to ever happen to me.'

Ellie breathed in sharply. Now it was her turn to say, 'Don't.'

'Don't what?'

'Say things you don't mean.'

'I've never been more serious in my life.' Niccolo was heartened by the flicker of emotion in her eyes, an instinctive reaction which she had not quite been able to conceal. 'I've never talked to anyone the way I talked to you. No one has ever made me laugh the way you did and I've never missed any woman the way I've missed you.'

'You didn't get in touch!' Ellie said accusingly.

'Every day was a struggle to stop myself from dialling your number.' He shot her a crooked smile. 'I kept telling myself that my life had to remain just the way it was. Straightforward and uncomplicated. My brief, from way back when, was to be the financial powerhouse that ensured the stability of my family unit—my mother, my sisters. I kept telling myself that I'd had a shot at a relationship and that particular arrow had spectacularly backfired—except, deep down, I wasn't convinced.'

He sighed and looked at her with open honesty. 'I almost had to stay at the opposite end of the world to safeguard the way of life I'd spent a lifetime building up, but of course that was never going to last. When I read your campaign, the longing to be with you was so overwhelming I found it hard to breathe. But even if I'd never read the pitch, never seen those pictures that reminded me of our time together, I would still have had to get in touch with you, Ellie. I had to come here. And not because I want to persuade you back into bed with me—although, naturally, that's part of the package. I would have had to come here because you wriggled your way into my heart and into my soul and became part of me without me even realising.'

'I did? Niccolo...don't tease. What package?'

'Oh.' His voice shook with the nerves of someone peering into the deep well of an abyss. 'The whole love and marriage package.'

'Sorry?' Ellie's eyes widened. Her heart skipped a beat.

'I love you, Ellie, and I want to marry you. I never thought I'd say those words to anyone but I can't imagine a life without you in it. I had three weeks of that and it was hell.'

'You love me?' The hope she had been trying her best to stifle blossomed, swelled and filled her and she smiled, tremulously at first, and then with absolute joy. 'I love you too,' she whispered. 'But then you knew that.' She wriggled towards him and then linked her arms behind his neck and nestled into him, hearing the steady beat of his heart and placing her small hand over it with a wave of love and tenderness.

'I've been miserable,' she confessed, tilting her face to his and then reaching up to kiss him on his lips. 'I didn't even care that my job had gone, even though it was the most important thing in my life. Nothing mattered any more. I was rudderless for the first time. That's why I was heading back home. I spent my whole life wishing that I had normal parents who did normal things but I knew that, if anyone was going to understand what I was going through, it would be them.

'I always thought that their lives were chaotic and disorganised and filled with people who didn't seem to have any ties, who kept coming and going. I didn't see beyond that to the fact that, among all that chaos, they loved one another. I thought that if I didn't exercise control and get things *just right* I would end up falling into a life of chaos and I'd somehow be lost. I didn't see that love can't be controlled, and that what looks as though it promises chaos can be the one thing that makes the most sense. I love you so much, Niccolo.'

Her voice trembled and he held her close against him.

'However much we travel,' he murmured, 'whatever oceans we cross, my darling, I will always be your rock and your point of reference. I've discovered that that's all I want to do. You're the centre of my life, and I will give you all the stability you wanted as a child. Just as you have given me the confidence to trust in a future where there's love and to let go all the fears that were cemented in me as a child, that love and duty could never join hands. I adore you, Ellie, and if I could take back one thing it would be my bull-headed stubbornness that made me let you go. So will you, Ms Eleanor Wilson of the late and not lamented starchy navy suits, be my lawfully wedded wife and promise to be by my side for the rest of our days?'

Ellie smiled and beamed at him. 'Just try and stop me...'

* * * * *

Get 2 Free Books,
Plus 2 Free Gifts—
just for trying the Reader Service!

YES! Please send me 2 FREE Harlequin® Romance Larger-Print novels and my 2 FREE gifts (gifts are worth about $10 retail). After receiving them, if I don't wish to receive any more books, I can return the shipping statement marked "cancel." If I don't cancel, I will receive 4 brand-new novels every month and be billed just $5.34 per book in the U.S. or $5.74 per book in Canada. That's a savings of at least 15% off the cover price! It's quite a bargain! Shipping and handling is just 50¢ per book in the U.S. and 75¢ per book in Canada*. I understand that accepting the 2 free books and gifts places me under no obligation to buy anything. I can always return a shipment and cancel at any time. The free books and gifts are mine to keep no matter what I decide.

119/319 HDN GMWL

Name _____ (PLEASE PRINT)

Address _____ Apt. #

City _____ State/Prov. _____ Zip/Postal Code

Signature (if under 18, a parent or guardian must sign)

Mail to the **Reader Service:**

IN U.S.A.: P.O. Box 1341, Buffalo, NY 14240-8531
IN CANADA: P.O. Box 603, Fort Erie, Ontario L2A 5X3

Want to try two free books from another line?
Call 1-800-873-8635 or visit www.ReaderService.com.

*Terms and prices subject to change without notice. Prices do not include applicable taxes. Sales tax applicable in N.Y. Canadian residents will be charged applicable taxes. Offer not valid in Quebec. This offer is limited to one order per household. Books received may not be as shown. Not valid for current subscribers to Harlequin Romance Larger-Print books. All orders subject to approval. Credit or debit balances in a customer's account(s) may be offset by any other outstanding balance owed by or to the customer. Please allow 4 to 6 weeks for delivery. Offer available while quantities last.

Your Privacy—The Reader Service is committed to protecting your privacy. Our Privacy Policy is available online at www.ReaderService.com or upon request from the Reader Service.

We make a portion of our mailing list available to reputable third parties that offer products we believe may interest you. If you prefer that we not exchange your name with third parties, or if you wish to clarify or modify your communication preferences, please visit us at www.ReaderService.com/consumerschoice or write to us at Reader Service Preference Service, P.O. Box 9062, Buffalo, NY 14240-9062. Include your complete name and address.

Get 2 Free Books,
<u>Plus</u> 2 Free Gifts –

just for
trying the
**Reader
Service!**

Get 2 Free Books,
Plus 2 Free Gifts—
just for trying the Reader Service!